Thinner than a Hair

Adnan Mahmutović

Published by Cinnamon Press
Meirion House,
Glan yr afon,
Tanygrisiau,
Blaenau Ffestiniog,
Gwynedd,
LL41 3SU.
www.cinnamonpress.com

The right of Adnan Mahmutović to be identified as the author of this work has been asserted by him in accordance with the Copyright, Designs and Patent Act, 1988. © Adnan Mahmutović 2010. ISBN 978-1-907090-03-5
British Library Cataloguing in Publication Data. A CIP record for this book can be obtained from the British Library
All rights reserved. No part of this publication may be reproduced, stored in a retrieval system, or transmitted in any form or by any means, electronic, mechanical, photocopying, recording or otherwise without the prior written permission of the publishers. This book may not be lent, hired out, resold or otherwise disposed of by way of trade in any form of binding or cover other than that in which it is published, without the prior consent of the publishers.

All the characters in this book are fictitious and any resemblance to actual persons, living or dead, is purely coincidental.

Designed and typeset in Garamond by Cinnamon Press. Cover design by Mike Fortune-Wood from original artwork 'Pocitelj Mosque' by Salahudin, agency: dreamstime.com. Printed in Poland.

Cinnamon Press is represented in the UK by Inpress Ltd www.inpressbooks.co.uk and in Wales by the Welsh Books Council www.cllc.org.uk.

for Merima

Thinner than a Hair

Prologue
(Munich 2001)

Even dew is heavy in Dachau. When water drops roll down the strands of grass and disappear in cracked soil, the grass vibrates like strings of my father's *shargija*, which he used only when singing old Bosnian songs of love and religion. Every morning, I'd follow my father's tradition to step out barefoot across our lawn, stand squinting in the cold sunshine, then collect the dew in the deltas of my palms, and wash my face as if performing the Muslim ritual before the first prayer.

I press my palms against the damp cellar wall, trying to feel the dew and hear the singing grass. This morning, I hide like I did in 1993 in my motherland, my ears cocked for the sound of barking German shepherds, and police sirens. The immigration officers are coming for me today. I can feel it; it'll happen today, on Valentine's day.

To stop thinking about handcuffs and boisterous German voices, I break my nail clipper carving my name in the wall: Fatima. I speak out loud, but not too loud, 'Mum, Dad, Aziz, please forgive me. I should never have left you. I have been the worst daughter, the nastiest lover.'

Daughter, lover, illegal immigrant, and now, a broke prostitute. How in God's name have I managed to do this? As if I'm a pebble that a boy once flung across a river and it only touched the water in four places.

My mind seems to have packed and hidden away most of my growing up and my innocence, as if there never was any, as if I've always been twenty-six. At this moment, thinking of where I am and what I do for a living, it's hard to believe that a whore could once have been a child, a virgin, a different person altogether. Or perhaps not altogether, perhaps just a little bit different. Can I revisit another time and place without bringing along who I am now? Can I rerun some past love in my head without, at the moment, being in the mood for love? I can't decide whether everything I went through was a long preparation for who I am. Our local imam once said, 'Everything's written and if God plays dice with us,' here he whispered words of repentance, as if for a sin committed, 'then they might be loaded.' But fate's a different kind of writing. It's getting the whole package delivered at birth that makes my life one grand project of opening all the small boxes inside the big one. In the end, when I've unwrapped everything, all smells, paints, tints, textures and gestures, there will hardly be enough left of me to scare all the stray crows come to pick at my bones when I'm dead.

I know how I was born. Father must have told me a thousand times in his strong mild voice. Mum gave me her version too, but I like Father's better.

Every Woman is a Faith
(Summer 1974)

A woman's bones go out of joint in labour, my mum used to say. In Bosnia, tradition prescribes that a woman rest for forty days and nights before jumping back to her chores. Minding the baby is quite enough. That worked well for my mother back in 1974, in the Bosnian countryside. She followed the tradition, even though she was a damn house-proud woman. She'd whitewash the inner walls of the house every couple of months. Even her friends with heavy-smoking husbands said anything more than twice a year was nothing short of madness, especially in wintertime. Mum would look at the impeccable walls, her skin pores full of lime, proud like a patriot before a flag, chanting her favourite proverb, 'The house rests on a woman and not on the ground.'

I didn't fall into the world on some politically significant day or night, at a cut in the country's history like that Indian boy Saleem I read about in literature class. I was born on Midsummer Day 1974, through an incision made to enlarge my mother's opening. I was not washed by patriotic tears, but by maternal tears caused by terrible labour pains, because I was coming out butt-first. She never stopped reminding me of that, saying to me, 'I thought I was going to explode. You took twenty hours to come out. They cut me and pulled you out with this metal thing. I screamed. I thought your head was going to fall off.' But that wasn't the whole deal. I was pulled out first, and my twin brother fell victim to my urge to be first. I paved his way yet cut off his breath with my umbilical cord. The nurses took me out of the room and washed me with hot water. I still have burn marks, map-like patches of slightly darker skin on my neck, back, and behind. Then they wrapped me in cotton nappies and tightened my entire body with a long linen belt to make my body straight and strong. Finally, they separated me from Mum for three days. Once Mum had recovered enough for breastfeeding, they brought me back. I looked like a well-wrapped loaf of bread with a reddish, burnt crust in white paper.

It would take seventeen years for Mum to tell me about my Gemini. I wonder what he was like? Perhaps he was the mirror image of me.

'You were the most beautiful baby in the world, little rainbow,' Father always said. He told me other things too, which I put together in my head like a short film. I was only a few weeks old, but my parents' stories were so vivid that it was as though I had my own magical memories. My mind filled in details, things I imagine must have happened, my parents' feelings, the subtle movements of their faces and bodies, the smells in the air. Everything is there, and it feels great, imagining my own origin, re-inventing that single moment of innocence. I've earned the right to some nostalgia.

On a cool August dawn, after my mother's forty-day period, I was suckling her. As she lay beside me, I imagine she was thinking of the first thing she'd have to do the following day. Two months earlier, in anticipation of the babe, my father had whitewashed the whole house and it had the uncanny smell of home.

That morning he pushed open the screen door to the veranda. A cool draught brought in the thick, bittersweet smell of painted wood from the newly painted fence Father had put up so I wouldn't fall out once I began to walk. He yelled out to my mother, 'Come on, Safija! You have to see this.'

Mum rose up, nagging as much as her early-morning, pre-coffee energy levels allowed, 'Yeah, yeah, I'm coming. Don't you see what I'm doing? I got up three hours before you. This girl's just hungry all the time, but she won't take the nipple. Maybe I have no milk left. I just don't know…'

She wanted to show that Father wasn't the one who gave the orders. Even if she always did as he said, she at least made sure she was still in charge of the spoken word.

She pulled up her black silk skirt, straightened her tired back, pinched the nipple that I'd let go of with her thumb and forefinger, and stuffed it back into my mouth, pressing my head against her breast. She went out to the veranda, looked down at me and said, 'Just like that. Stop wriggling and grab it.'

The veranda was like an extra room, but roofless, with a thick trellis over large peacock-cushions and a low table. Mum shuddered. 'It's suddenly getting rather chilly out here. I should've wrapped a cardigan around my back. You know how my kidneys are when it breezes cold outside.'

'Stop talking and look up.'

She opened her mouth, as she always did when stunned by something. It was the largest, clearest shimmering rainbow she had ever seen.

I began to cry and Mum kissed me on the forehead and caressed my blond, curly hair to make me stop, never for a second taking her eyes off the sky. Father turned back and his eyes squinted at the sight of a tuft of glistening hair sticking out from the blue-white baby cover. He closed in on me, kissed my hair and cheek, and smelled the faint scent. My ear was folded, the cloth on my head pressing it from behind. He set it right and kissed it.

'Leave her be!' Mum moved back from him. 'Can't you see she's eating?'

The rainbow wheedled other people out of their homes as well. Whole families from the smallest to the biggest houses on the slope were gathered on their verandas or in their yards, looking at this marvel, which erased doubt, fear, discontent, and downbeat sentiments. The all-embracing enchantment was interrupted by laughter. Impossible to say from which direction the peals echoed. The words, 'Look, Nisveta's trying to walk under the rainbow!' sounded sonorously from all kinds of voices. The mute dawn became a nonsensical chattering.

Nisveta was an old, childless, epileptic woman who had a stone-deaf husband. She had burn scars all over her face, arms, and even breasts. When Nisveta collapsed with spasms while carrying a cauldron of smouldering laundry, or fell on hot iron plates, it could take hours before her deaf man found her. Nisveta was testing the old Bosnian myth that walking under a rainbow would change the sex of the person who does it. I don't think she believed it. Rather than becoming a man, maybe she just wanted to be something other than who she was.

To the people watching, to strive for the irrational was a sign of a withering mind and an inflamed heart. Fools, they can't see the rain for the water, let alone the rainbow for all the colours. In those telephoneless times, the news of Nisveta's desperate measures travelled faster than Nisveta's bandy legs could carry her. Then a self-proclaimed tell-all, an old-fashioned tidings-bringer, ended up under our veranda, yelling himself hoarse, broadcasting in an old-fashioned way, 'Nisveta's trying to walk under the rainbow! Silly, silly woman! The heat melted her brain!'

'Oh, shut up!' Father cried at him. 'You're making a fool of yourself!' Father's seven-foot stature and his scornful gaze, topped by a pair of black and bushy eyebrows were not threatening to the man, who just leered back. The man pulled up his scuffed trousers, which were tied with a piece of rope, patted his green cap backwards, sniffed over his moustache, and dashed away, indulging his newly discovered talent.

Father turned away and came close to Mum. He embraced her and kissed her on the lips.

'Your moustache is wet.' She pressed her lips together, handed me to him, put her breast back into the blouse, and wiped her mouth dry with her sleeve.

He bit his lip. A line crossed his forehead and he squinted. He turned away and hoisted my little body. 'Look,

Fatima, a rainbow! You see the beautiful colours? There are seven of them, you know.' Father, such a romantic.

'Don't bother,' Mum said. 'She's too tiny to see anything. Babies can only see their mothers and nothing else. Especially not their fathers.'

'She can see me all right.'

I yawned. He lowered his gaze from me and saw a panting woman leaned on a pile of chopped wood under the veranda. 'Safija, look, there's Nisveta.' Nisveta looked up. He said, 'Come over here. Safija will make us a pot in a moment.'

Mum rolled her eyes.

Nisveta said, 'Don't bother, my dear. I've already had a cup with Suljo. He gets up so early he even wakes the rooster.'

Father said, 'Let's have another one then. Such a nice morning. Shame to run for work right away.'

Nisveta took another look at the shimmering bridge, which seemed to have moved farther away with every step she'd taken closer to it. 'You're right.'

Mum said, 'Rasim, let her in, I'll put the kettle on.'

Nisveta came up the outdoor stairs that led to the upper part of the house. It was built into the slope of a hill and the rear windows of the second storey faced the woods. Those in front were turned to the open space of the valley, so my family could see the whole town, and the small river Bobas speeding down into the slow flowing river, Vrbanja. Nisveta supported herself on the red façade bricks. It was a new countryside vogue, instead of a cement façade. She faced the heavy front door, and a half-opaque, round window through which she could see the contorted shadow of my father. She sighed. The door opened.

'I'm sorry for bothering you this early□'

'Don't be silly. Come on in.' Mum greeted Nisveta with a big smile, but was a little anxious to remove me from the sight of the tired woman. 'Let me just put this little nuisance to bed. She can ruin your coffee break before you know what hit you.'

'She's a beauty, *mashallah*.'

'She is, but she's giving me trouble already. God knows what'll happen when she gets older.'

'I'm sure she'll be fine, *inshallah*. Can I hold her?'

'She's a nuisance, really.'

Mum was actually afraid I would be affected by the evil eye of the unexpected visitor, afraid that the fate of the troubled woman would transfer onto the fragile little me. Still, she knew it'd be rude to refuse a childless mother. 'I'll put her here on the sofa and you can keep an eye on her, will you? I'll be right back.' Mum put me on my special quilt and disappeared behind the oak kitchen door. Father was on his way into the room, but he stopped and stood silently watching Nisveta. She grabbed me, held me up against her face and pressed her half-burnt lips on my forehead. Father went out to give her a moment. Raindrops hit windows. I shrieked. Mum and Father ran back in. Nisveta was lying on the floor next to me.

Heat
(Spring 1986)

The scar on my left cheekbone is in the shape of a scimitar. It itches when it's cold and sometimes it hurts before a hot day turns into a rainy evening. It's like a signal, a sixth sense. But it never warned me of my mother's mood changes, which became more frequent than weather changes.

A week before my twelfth birthday, Mum woke up before the rooster crowed and shook us awake. 'Get up sleepyheads,' she cried cheerfully. 'Let's make this place shine.'

Father and I just looked at each other as we ambled to the bathroom to wash our faces. Father said, 'Not whitewashing again. Come on Safija, this is crazy.'

Mum said, 'Hush now and hurry up, will you.' She was already rolling carpets, pushing heavy lockers from the walls, taking off pictures, and covering sofas with huge nylon sheets to protect them from the lime.

I sat on the toilet longer than I needed. Mum opened the door, quickly scowled at me because I was still not dressed, and then she smiled to show how excited she was about the cleaning spree. God, that was weird, I thought. The smell of slaked lime from the bucket she was holding cleared my head. I was ready.

Mum made me put on my torn jeans, which I always wanted to wear to school, but which she hated. She didn't get what the big deal was with torn jeans.

A brush in my right hand, I jumped on the kitchen table and applied lime to the ceiling. I had a wet cloth in my left to wipe off lime that dripped on my face. My scar itched and I scratched it.

Father, who was working the walls, smiled, pointed at my scar, and said, 'You only need a hammer.' The crossed scimitar and the hammer made the symbol of the working class, the communist heroes. I put my fist against my temple, as all famous heroes did in those bleached pictures on the walls in my school, and I started to mock-sing the national anthem. Father wasn't really a communist but everyone was in the party back then. He didn't want to be an exception, some sort of a secular heretic. He laughed at my singing. Then he signalled to me with his eyes and said, 'Let's check on your mother.'

She was doing my room. Her hand movements were not clumsy like mine. She was the Rembrandt of whitewashing, of housekeeping. When she saw us standing in the doorway and smiling at her, she shook her brush and spruced us with lime. 'You've had your fun watching me, so get back to work. It's her birthday next week and I want this house to be ready for it.'

I wanted to say I didn't really care, that the house was just fine, and besides no one was coming. It'd be just the three of us, and a huge cake without candles. Before I went back to work, I said, 'Can I have candles this year? Like in the American films?'

She knitted her brows. 'You know I hate candles. Candles are for churches, for the dead people.'

'But we're not Christians.'

'Exactly.'

No candles this year either.

We finished the whitewashing late in the afternoon, left all the windows open so the walls would dry faster, and so that the pungent smell wouldn't sink into the sofas. In the evening, after we'd eaten crumbled cornbread in hot milk, Mum made some coffee for Father and herself, and chamomile tea with bitter chestnut honey for me. She hardly said a word. As if having a coffee break would be an inexcusable loss of time, she took to crocheting. Father and I kept rolling our eyes at her. We sipped our beverages hot. Mum waited for her coffee to cool. Then she put the handiwork down, looked at the walls, sighed with great pleasure, drank her coffee in one swig, kissed us both on our heads, and went to the stable to milk the cow and the goat.

Father said, 'Let me do it, you're tired.'

'Ah, don't bother. Enjoy your coffee.'

He yawned and said, 'I think I'll just go to sleep.'

I too could hardly keep my eyes open. I said, 'I think I'll just wash myself and go to sleep too.'

Mum said nothing and went out with a plastic bucket. Father just smiled at me, kissed me and went to his bedroom. I watched Mum flashing her lamp at the darkness and then she disappeared behind the stable door. The moon was new.

My stomach hurt and I sat on the toilet for half an hour before I felt better. Then, I practically flooded the bathroom washing my feet in the shower. Mum hated to see me squander water, but I loved feeling and watching water glide down my naked legs. I could do it for hours. I bowed to rub my feet, and felt like a cut in my stomach again. Warm blood ran down my thighs. I was a prolific bleeder even from that first time. I hunched. The liquid circled around my feet. I tried to scream, but I had no voice. I slipped, falling down into the blood that smelled like fish.

I sat there, watching my own blood slowly run away from my naked legs and disappearing under the bathtub, into the drainage system. I heard the door open and slam. It was Mum. I didn't try to call her in case she punished me for what I'd done, even though I had no idea what it was I'd done.

I tried to stand up, but my limbs glided from under me like in the Bambi cartoon. I hit my chin against the basin and finally cried. Mum rushed in, still holding a bucketful of milk. Her eyes bulged as she screamed, 'Fatima, what happened?' She dropped the bucket on the tiles close to me. The foamy, fat milk washed the blood away.

My voice was back. 'I don't know, I don't know. I think I cut myself.'

Mum knew it wasn't a cut. She grabbed a small towel and put it between my legs. 'Don't worry, it's fine. It's nothing dangerous. Let's go to my room and I'll tell you everything.' Then she wrapped me in a large towel, and carried me away to her huge bed. Father was already snoring on his side of the bed, rolled in a thick quilt. He jumped up when she kicked him with her knee. 'Rasim, get out! Go sleep on the sofa!'

'What's the matter? Is she all right?'

'Just leave.'

Father left, but too slowly, ambling out backward, watching me shiver in Mum's arms. He took time closing the door, while Mum was putting me down. She hollered, 'Close the door!'

Mum whispered things I didn't understand, but the tone was thick and slow like dollops of apple syrup dropping on my morning bread. She lay down next to me and pulled me to her self. She opened her blouse and pressed her warm body against me. She smelled of her usual sweat, and musty cow smell too, but that didn't matter at all. My God, how nice those animals smelled that moment on Mum, like the best perfume. Her body was hot as the simmering Bosnian casserole she made on weekends. She failed to smile before she said, 'You're a woman now. God help you.'

That was when I started to love heat and hate cold. The next day was Sunday, the day we used to bathe. Mum heated up huge tin vessels on the stove, threw clove and bits of dried apples on the plates so the fumes smelled fresh and tickly in the nose. She scrubbed me first, while Father shaved himself. I just hunched in the shower and she rubbed in my hair this dark smelly soap she used for clothes, because she'd heard it was good for hair growth. There was no blood. It took time to remove the lime from my face and forearms. Then, while I was blow-drying my hair, she rubbed the soap into Father's hair and his back, which was covered with all shapes of birthmarks. She bathed him like a babe, though his huge body could hardly fit into the shallow tub. I stood wrapped in a towel, leaning on the doorframe and laughing when she poured hot water over his head and rubbed, rubbed, rubbed. God, that was a great life.

Cold
(Autumn 1989)

With the passing years, as Mum lost her heat, the house grew colder and colder, even when the air outside was dusty and sweaty. It even smelled cold. I never forgave Mum for losing her smells. I missed the heat of her skin. She was that age when she was losing her period, one moment freezing then sweating like a heifer.

She washed and ironed starched white-red needlework on carved tables every day. She laid oriental carpets wall-to-wall, put up shelves full of brass tablets with engravings of cultural heritage, mementos bought at Bascarsija market in Sarajevo. Lace curtains at the windows dispersed light like loose clouds. More laced cloths lay over soft couches. Yet it looked as if nobody lived there—just nicely arranged to be photographed for one of those calendars that all Bosnian refugees and *Gastarbeiters* (foreign guest workers) kept on their kitchen walls in Germany to remind them of the beautiful homeland.

When I was fifteen, I hung a wooden plaque over the front door with an inscription: A Bosnian room. An exemplary living space of the exemplary population as it was preserved in the rural heart of the land. Don't touch! For a guided tour, ask the sulky attendant.

That same day, my father, coming back home tired and in a bad mood, found the broken plaque and guffawed. I didn't tell him Mum had smashed it against the doorframe trying to slap me across my back with it. She cringed in a corner when he laughed, wrapping a red-and-yellow wool quilt around her legs. She wouldn't look him in the eyes, just stared at his boots and the dirty snow he had not shaken off before coming inside.

Mum was quite illiterate, but pestered me about education. Once Mum tried to shake me awake an hour before school. The previous night, when I was sure they'd been snoring for an hour, I'd sneaked out of my room to watch an old Charlie Chaplin film, the one when he eats his own shoe and laces. I knew it was just film magic, but it felt real, as if I was sitting with Charlie in the cold shed, breathing in the hot fumes of the cooked shoe. My mouth felt sticky with the heavy odour of the reeking leather and rubber. I sensed both the hot dish and the extreme cold, and Charlie being so sweet I could eat him alive.

In the morning, I just couldn't get up. Mum threw some clothes over my head to make a point, but that didn't bother me at all, instead the clothes prevented the sunlight from tickling my itching eyes. Mum came in two more times to shout, 'School starts at eight!' Finally, at ten to eight, she scooped me up and threw me out of the house all ruffled and messy. It was snowing outside, and my bad breath billowed from my mouth in the form of small clouds. While I dusted the dirt from my knees, she hurled my jeans bag after me with a volley of garbled words. I could have spent the day hiding in the little shed farther uphill but I knew Mum would check with the teachers and make an even worse fuss, so I went to school. In my damn pyjamas. I was in the spotlight, getting all the world's laughs, for another six months. It all stopped when a boy peed in his trousers when we dissected frogs in the biology class. I was free and anonymous.

I learned my first foreign language with a private tutor a couple of years earlier than other kids did. In most Bosnian schools, we had Russian and German. Ever since sovereign Tito had died, Russian was on its way out like an emaciated dog with its tail between its hind legs. 'The language of Communism,' as Father said with a sneer. 'No use if we're not going to live in the USSR. German, the language of *Gastarbeiters*; that's what you should learn.' He obviously didn't know German was the mother tongue of the father of Communism. We had Marxism on the curriculum in high school.

Since I had German in school, I begged Father to let me learn English. He agreed to do it, even though it cost him a lot. I think it's remarkable that a small-town girl learned such disparate languages, just so she might stand a chance if she ever needed to flee the country. We didn't know which language was going to dominate the world. That's called learning from history–that tomorrow might bring anything.

In the beginning, English was cool to learn, but at times it was a pain in the tongue and I hated it. The tutor, who was this prim little figure with Woody Allen glasses and greasy hair said, 'I guess the English would hate our mother tongue too.'

I said, 'But to hate it, they'd have to be forced to learn it. There's no chance that'll ever happen.'

'In English, please,' he said, and pushed up his glasses.

I scratched my head in a few erratic movements. He smiled, and said, in what he called the royal accent, 'All right, young lady. I'll read and you'll listen. It doesn't matter if you don't understand immediately; it's the sound you need to sense first. Now just relax and listen. This book is famous. Its title is *Emma* and it was written by an English small-town girl, like you.'

'Is it romantic?'

'I suppose so. Yes, it's romantic. Anyway, this woman, Jane, never married.'

'Just like you.'

He went silent for a moment, hawked, and then said, 'Right, then, people imagine this spinster hardly ever left her home. She wrote beautiful and amusing, but bitter stories about a kind of high-class peasantry. Now Emma's the heroine.'

'A girl?'

'Blonde and fair like you.'

'But no scar.'

He muted. His lips stretched and turned to brass over his teeth. He was like a well-wrought sculpture with an uncanny spark of life in it. He grabbed my shoulders, kissed the thin lime-white line on my cheek and said in a mild tone, 'Not a scar; a sign, a symbol.' Then he kissed me a dozen more times on it, as if my scar had some healing power for him. I was stunned. After that, it was good he wanted me to listen to his reading instead of practicing conversation, because I couldn't say one word. He avoided my eyes the rest of the session.

He pulled that stunt many times in the following six months and our tutorials became longer and longer, until one beautiful day Mum wafted into the room, forgetting about the lecture. The teacher was holding my head between his hands and kissing my chin. Mum went out coolly, as if nothing had happened. The man rose, peered out of the door, and then cried, 'Hey! What the hell?' The four-foot long wooden stick Mum used to make sheets of dough for pastry passed an inch from his eyes. He ran off, Mum chasing him. I dashed after them. It was such fun, like in Charlie Chaplin's old films. The man miscalculated and thought he could escape through the veranda door, but the height made him dizzy, and Mum barged him from the other side and over the fence.

In the end, they found me a woman.

Inez, my new and the last private teacher, was a robust woman, fierce-looking until she smiled. A smile completely transformed her naturally knit brows and hanging face into a collage of beautiful, thin wrinkles. When she smiled or laughed she did it with her entire body. I loved her flowery dresses and her swaying accent. I told her so and she explained it to me, 'My vowels are thicker and mustier.'

I had no idea what that meant, but it sure sounded nice. I showed her my Jane Austen books and she waved her hand. 'Enough of that washed out, tense spinsterhood. You need to read real literature. Men.'

I stared into her big brown eyes. 'Men?'

She blew her messy bleached hair from her eyes. 'Men, and women of course, but more,' here she made a gesture of grabbing and squeezing something, 'more forceful, you know what I mean?'

I didn't even blink.

She said, 'Yes, modern stuff, with more sex.'

'Sex.'

'Yes, people eating each other up, sucking each other dry, holding one another tight, kissing, kissing, kissing.'

I kept still, thinking, Mum must never know what we do here. My God, and she thought that man meant trouble. I said, 'You will teach me sex?'

'No, and yes, of course not. I won't show you, you know, sex. I will teach you the history of Eros,'

'Who's Eros?'

She flailed with her arms and tapped me on the cheek. 'There you go, you'll be a fine student I can see. You ask good questions.'

She never explained who or what Eros was, because she spent many hours rambling about her old lovers and conquests. I prayed to God Mum didn't hear Inez talking, because her voice set the room vibrating. I thought she'd melt the floor and fall down through the ceiling onto Mum's neck, down in the kitchen.

Inez said, 'We'll start with the first woman writer in history. An Arab girl, Scherezade. Now that was a woman. There you have it all: sex, death, and war. And more sex.' She pulled out a swollen looking book. It was well preserved, but the pages looked greasy at the edges. Inez liked rubbing her fingers against the paper as she turned the pages. 'People have forgotten her. She's become an exotic mist.'

'You mean like a ghost.'

'Like a ghost, that's right girl, like a ghost, a spirit, a female Jinn.'

Inez kept me on edge, the way Scherezade did her king, always telling intriguing pieces, mysteries that were both solved and dissolved like sugar in milk. There were stories in stories in yet more stories. I was mostly confused, but always wondered what happened next, next, next.

I never found out if it was Inez's plan, a symbolic gesture, but she stayed with me exactly one hundred and one days, not a thousand and one. Since we only met on weekends, that meant almost two years. I was nearly seventeen when she left. We read Henry Miller together, and a horrible book I never understood called *The Naked Lunch*, which made my stomach turn. It was so difficult to read on my own, but she explained a lot of nasty stuff. I didn't see the point of that one.

One thing I remember best about her. She always had travel books with her. She had an album of pictures from *National Geographic*. On the hard cover of her album she'd glued a picture of a Gypsy-looking woman from Afghanistan with incredibly bright green eyes. Inside, on the very first page, there was a black and white photo of an Indian temple and some statues. I could not blink, or turn away, or say anything. Inez said, 'You like it?'

I nodded erratically.

'This will be your next written assignment, to describe these statues and how they make you feel.'

'Who—'

'No, don't ask anything just yet. I'll tell you after you're done.'

I cannot remember exactly what I wrote, how many language errors I made, but the picture was of four finely chiselled women, well proportioned, round as round can be without being fat. They had long necklaces over big breasts, and thick, smooth hair. They were all naked and I couldn't understand how it was possible to look so natural yet contorted. One woman was standing on her head with both her hands covering the crotches of the two women standing by her sides. The fourth woman's legs were entwined with the one upside-down and their vaginas were pressed against each other. They were made of stone, but looked so alive, smooth, and tactile, so sexually laden; I felt my body vibrating. I didn't know what to do with myself. Even the following day, while Inez explained those were not loose women, my body was playing tricks on me. I imagined touching the statues, the women coming to life and grabbing me and dragging along into huge dark forests.

'What are they?'

'I believe they were priestesses.'

I gaped back at her as if I understood what it meant. I'd never seen a priestess.

'These are nearly a thousand years old.'

'A thousand and one,' I said and she smiled. The following weekend she kissed me goodbye and left, swaying her huge bottom down our street. Mum said it was strange Inez forgot her last month's payment. I kept struggling with the Indian women in my dreams for a few more nights and then they disappeared back into the jungle as if they were never discovered in the first place.

Humming Peasant
(Autumn 1991)

I was seventeen when I spotted Aziz masturbating in our cornfield. He was seven years older, and just as inexperienced with the opposite sex. The sun was in a giving vein. The corn stalks were like an array of translucent elves, turned to all sides of the world in a noon prayer. Slowly, the valley became a blaze. Wafts of warm wind rustled over the long, sharp leaves. I couldn't hear my own steps or the cracking sounds of my naked arms brushing against the corn. I guess that was why Aziz never noticed me in the first place.

He lay in a small clearing in the field, humming old crooner songs. He had his left hand in his trousers. The sun hit his eyes and he stood up. His bony cheeks disappeared in the light with the rest of his tall body, like a distant mirage. Then he reappeared. His hair became darker and wavier as he sweated. He pulled his hand out of his slack trousers and wiped the sweat off his swollen nose. He looked at the sky, scowled and sneezed. He pressed one nostril with his thumb and blew several times. Then he dried his face with his soiled shirt and hastily looked around. I stood like a scarecrow. Some perverse part of me hoped he'd notice me and I'd exchange a word with our best worker, The Humming Peasant, as I called him.

Aziz tore a handful of corn silk, wrested off the sunburnt tops, and slowly fell to his knees. The soil was cracked. He peered again over both his shoulders and, satisfied that he was alone, his right hand slipped through the open zipper. He wrapped the corn silk around his penis and clutched it. He jerked it for a minute in a downward movement and then bit his upper lip as his prick swelled and rose up out of the trousers. He rubbed it hard and unrhythmically – harder and faster, until the silk was drenched and he toppled, panting and crying.

Aziz wept a short while and let go of the dripping penis. He dried himself with a couple of long corn leaves. The brittle edge of a leaf cut the shrivelled skin and he merely looked at his fingers, zipped his trousers back, rose and shuffled through the corn towards the woodshed where we kept the tools locked. I took the opposite way. A street opened itself before me and I went up to the woodshed. As I came closer, a voice cut right through me, 'Oh, *merhaba* Aziz.' It was Father. I was stiff. 'So you're already here, good. Have you seen my daughter? She said she'd be here, waiting for the workers. Has anybody else come?'

Aziz wiped his palms against his trousers before shaking hands with Father but said nothing. He watched me coming towards them, shaking bits of leaves from my clothes. I didn't care if he suspected I'd seen him. I thought, Damn, that was a bold move. Masturbating in another man's field. I wondered if he liked the thrill, but he appeared so damn innocent and crassly dull.

While I studied him, he just went on looking at me. Not a bit confused. I expected him to be surprised, as if he'd discovered a new continent – a flat, meagre, yet enticing landscape.

Father said, 'What are you looking at?' He turned to see me standing there. 'Ah, Fatima, it's you. Did you meet Aziz?'

'No.' Aziz didn't attempt to shake hands with me. I said, 'Nobody else is here.'

'I guess it's my fault. It's too damn hot.'

Aziz said, 'I told you it's better to start early in the morning.'

'Guess you're right, lad. My fault. Could you tell everybody on the way home? I count on you.'

'Sure.'

'If they can't make it, then come back and tell me. If you don't return, I assume it's all settled, then.'

'Okay.'

Aziz left. He didn't stumble over a stone or suddenly step into a hole in the road in that sweet way blokes get clumsy when they see someone they like. He walked away casually and without a trace of shame or nervousness. Was he stupid, or just terribly confident and daring? I had no idea. I could hardly think, or keep a straight face. The cheeky bastard. He got me there.

I spent more than a month thinking about Aziz. Father hired him at least ten times since our first meeting, to help picking the plums we sold to people who made brandy called *sljivovica*, which Mum hated, so Father never distilled any himself.

Quite on purpose, I would hide in some place where Aziz could easily see me if he ever lifted his head from work. He did a couple of times, but shyly turned his head away. The ice was still hard to break, despite the heat. Once he smiled, I melted.

When he helped with the potato field, he sometimes threw the tools away and unearthed potatoes with his bare hands, letting the soil crumble and fall through his fingers. He rubbed some smaller potatoes clean against his trousers and munched them, raw and hard as they were. My mouth shrank and contorted at the mere sight, but then became watery. I could feel his pleasure in this strange habit. Aziz kept surprising me. I felt like I'd known him for years and I knew he'd never dare ask me out on a date so I decided to take things into my own hands. That felt so good, making my first real decision.

On an unusually warm October day, I bribed a local boy with a chocolate bar to give Aziz a message to meet me on the only wooden bridge in town, the Rainbow Bridge. Its small arch is supposedly built in the exact place where many years before little rainbows appeared above the waterfalls.

We sat alone, peering down into the frothing hole where the mountain river disappeared like a water snake, to reemerge a few miles away. I was thinking about everything I normally couldn't care less about, that the stones and pebbles were freezing down there and that the planks were not comfortable.

Aziz's warm breath was all over my face. It smelled of mint, even though he had no chewing gum or sweets in his mouth. He heaved a deep breath through his nostrils and leaned over a bit too much, his forehead almost touching my thin thighs. A strong bramble smell tickled my nose, although it was no longer spring. There was the smell of compote with pears, plums, and quince; roasted nuts in dry prunes; lilac; simmering milk poured over white honey; hot bread releasing woolly plumes when dipped in thick apple syrup. All the things I loved. I raised my brows and opened my lids wide, as if to wake up. I knew there were no such smells around and I must've been imagining them. Those were the smells of home, the smells of different seasons. I thought he must have triggered them in me somehow. I wondered how he was feeling but didn't dare ask. Slipping my hand under his was less awkward. He pressed my hand hard against his thigh. I didn't think he wanted to hurt me. It was an immediate reaction, like an instinct. It was painful but I didn't pull my hand back or yell or grimace. We sat like that, peering into the water for hours, needing no words.

Then a rusty Fiat passed slowly over the bridge almost pushing us down into the river. I inhaled some dust. I coughed and closed my eyes so I didn't see the men in the car. Unaffected by dust, Aziz said, 'He showed us three fingers.' Three outstretched fingers was a Serbian nationalist sign, an open proclamation of their belonging and politics, a provocation.

I said, 'I don't care.' I hated that stuff. We lived in the period of Bosnian history when even the way of being a child or the manner of falling in love was political in some way. The old Yugoslavia was falling apart. The countries that had once formed the Yugoslav union wanted their national independence back. It was a time of reforms, and democratic elections. I mostly tried to play dumb and skip engaging with politics, but it wasn't always possible.

Aziz said, 'Have you registered?'

'Registered what?'

'Your nationality. Everybody must do it.'

I never expected politics to intrude on my first date, to permeate our first words to each other. I felt so disappointed. My ears burnt as if I had fever. I wanted to hurl myself into the cold water.

I said, 'I have no idea. What did you register as?'

'Muslim.'

'But that's not a nationality, that's religion. You should have written Bosnian.'

'That's not possible, I think. People register as Serbs, Croats, Muslim, Jew, I don't know, maybe other things too. Your father surely did it for you.'

'Did he?'

'I'm sure. Everybody's registered.'

'He never said anything to me.'

I was so used to only watching Aziz in silence I was astounded by his words. His voice was shaky but he spoke as though he was in front of a class of pupils. He said, 'If you haven't, we could go to the city centre and you could do it yourself. We can eat at one of those bakeries that the Kosovo-Albanian people run. They have great cakes, and make cold lemonade in large glass machines that never stop mixing.'

His voice was high-pitched and thick at the same time. He talked with his lips rounded and open, even to say sounds like p, b, and m. I wriggled to make him think I wanted to get up and walk away from him. I said, 'Is this your way of inviting to me to a second date. It's not very romantic you know.'

'I'm sorry. That was stupid.'

I laughed. It slipped out of me, 'Don't worry. Let's do it. I love sweets.' I made another decision. Everything was happening so fast and I couldn't predict what was up next. All the knots in my belly were suddenly undone and I somehow knew I was no longer a tease, or somebody who plays with boys because she can. Something told me this was what being a real woman was like. I knew my feelings and what to do about them. I felt an urge to explore the city, and Aziz, and new territories. I smiled confidently.

He smiled back, a bit less tense. 'I can ask this fellow Elvis to give us a ride.'

Then the voice of reason slapped me. 'Damn, what will my parents say? There's no way they'll let me go with you, even though they know you. And it's too far to get back in time without raising any suspicions.'

'It's only half an hour ride by car. We don't have to stay the whole day.'

I stood up and assumed a thinking pose.

Aziz stuttered, 'I'll ask your parents.'

I smiled. 'No, I have to do it.' I leaned down and expected he'd meet me halfway. He didn't. He gaped back at me as if he had no idea what to do. I lost balance and fell into his arms. I almost knocked us both down into the river. Aziz pushed himself up and brought us both back onto the safe middle of the narrow bridge. I lifted my head a little and gave him a peck on the lips. He buried his unevenly shaved face under my chin and kissed my throat. That left a mark. We watched each other for some time. He looked so puzzled, as if he could not believe this was possible, as if it was the last thing in the world that would happen to him.

I never asked my parents. Mum pulled me back into the house one second before I disappeared behind the front door, on my way to see how Aziz planned the whole city excursion. 'What's that around your neck?' She pulled the blue-white silk scarf with which I hid the hickey. It tightened. I put my fingers between my throat and the scarf to avoid being choked. It was warm outside. I wore a pale blue skirt and a white blouse, long enough to cover the thin leather belt with its simple silvery buckle. My hair was combed as much as the rebellious locks would give way to a comb. My cheeks rouged.

'Where are you going?'

'Nowhere, just out with the girls.'

'Why do you wear this?' Mum pulled it again, but the scarf was not giving way.

'I just like it. What's wrong with that?'

'I was a girl once; so don't give me those lies. You're going to meet that peasant bloke we used to hire, huh? I've seen you watch him.' She pulled the scarf harder. The knot loosened and it glided past my cheek. I clutched my fingers around my own neck, feeling the weal. 'How about homework? I never see you grab a book anymore. This is your father's fault. He spoils you.'

Father came in and yelled, 'What's going on?' His arms were like branches over Mum. 'Is that how you treat her when I'm not around?' He turned to me. 'What is it?'

Mum yelled, 'She's going to meet Aziz.'

I said with a poignant patriotic tone of voice, 'We're only going to the city to register.'

Father shook his head and yelled, 'Are you mad?' This was the first time he used such a tone with me, so I wasn't sure what to say. I was petrified by the man I loved. 'Go to the city? With Aziz? To register? Are you out of your mind?'

I said, 'It's my duty to register and I'm old enough to have a boyfriend.'

Father turned away from us and let Mum do the dirty work.

She cried, 'You're not going anywhere. You're not old enough to register or have a boyfriend.'

'Yes I am.'

Father muttered, 'You're not going and that's it.' His words were cold, for the first time. My stomach hurt and I felt cold crawling up my shoulders. I ran to my room, locked the door, and put on all the sweaters and jackets I had. Then I wrapped myself in a quilt. Mum tried to open the door, knocked nervously, then angrily, then banged for a minute and then shut up and left. Everything turned so damn dramatic for no reason. As if I'd killed someone or ran away from home, or worse, got knocked up.

The following week we went on our city trip. The car this man Elvis came in was a wreck, but that didn't bother anyone. Bosnians were great believers in German diesel engines, especially the people's favourite, the VW Golf. And it was white. Elvis said, gaping at my breasts, 'Better than the one Richard Gere came in to fetch Julia Roberts.' *Pretty Woman* had obviously impressed Bosnians. Everybody was talking about that film.

Elvis wore Levi 501s, torn and fringed at the knees, and a short-sleeved shirt. He was not clean-shaven and shiny-faced like Aziz, who was dressed in jeans and a black T-shirt, looking thin and uncomfortable in the tight garments. Aziz had water-combed his hair, which made it thicken and curl as the warm breeze fanned it.

Aziz introduced me. As I was preparing to shake hands with Elvis, he took hold of my hand, pulled it up, bowed a little, and then kissed it. I pulled it back. He smiled, revealing two golden fangs and cavity-infested teeth in between, which he instinctively licked and said, 'There's going to be another passenger. He'll be here in a minute.'

We packed ourselves into the car, Aziz and I in the back. Then came a sleek man, dressed in white. If he weren't blond I'd take him for an Italian. He was as tall as my father, only he was thin. He winked at Aziz and then turned to me. 'Ciao Bella. I'm Damir.' The fresh cologne fit his style perfectly.

Aziz knit his brows and his face was darker. Elvis slapped Damir on the shoulder and said, 'Leave my passengers alone.'

'Hey, don't worry. I'm just teasing my old mate Aziz. He got himself a date.' He sighed and raised one eyebrow like that Dylan from Beverly Hills series. 'Wow, I mean wow. Good for you Aziz.'

Aziz's said, 'It's fine. Damir, this is Fatima.'

He said, 'Nice to meet you. You took me by surprise. I didn't know rural Bosnia had such beautiful girls. The girls I meet in the city are pretty worn-out.'

I had a feeling it would hurt Aziz if I started a friendly conversation with Damir so I just smiled a little. I had no idea why Aziz disliked Damir or the role he'd play later in my life.

We crammed ourselves into the car. Fifteen minutes of silence later, Elvis's Golf screamed to a stop at a wide bridge. Damir held the door for me. I thanked him without looking at him. I smiled at my first real date, and then looked down over the stone fence at the calm river surface. Above the left bank, there were remains of a hundreds-of-years-old Turkish building called Kastel. It rose almost directly from the river Vrbas. It was kidney shaped, with high walls overgrown with ivy and no roof. Aziz and I walked along the narrow bank between the water and the wall, underneath a row of willows with branches dipped in the steady stream, like the hair of that young widow from an old crooner song.

Damir leaned on the car looking at me. I waved. Damir said, 'Take care, Aziz.'

Aziz ignored him. As we walked from Kastel, I said, 'Who was that Aziz?'

'Just an old friend from military service. Never mind, that was years ago.'

I was even more intrigued, but didn't push him. We entered a huge bazaar with dozens of booths full of vegetables and dried meat, then toys and music cassettes, kitchen paraphernalia, and clothes. Cigarette bootleggers stood in the flood of people mumbling into the ears of passers-by, 'Original Marlboro, original Kent, Drina, you name it we have it.'

At the far end, there was a long, glass building. The opiate smell of old cheese coming from it was so strong I held my breath for as long at it took us to go up the thirty-nine steps. I counted the steps to stop worrying about my date, and at the top, I let out the long breath.

Aziz said, 'Are you all right?' He didn't try to touch my hands or remove my moist hair from my eyes.

I gasped. 'You didn't smell that stench? I felt like…' I wanted to say vomiting but didn't think it was very appetizing, in case we kissed later and he thought about nothing but that word.

'What? The cheese?'

'My God, yes, the cheese.'

'I've eaten worse.'

I sat down on the top, laughing and looking over the slowly moving crowds. There was a rhythm in the flow of customers as well as in the cacophony of voices. Though they were not aware of it, people formed lines, like colourful streaks on the cobbled market, turning and spinning, getting tangled and untangled.

Aziz stood beside me, his left hand trembling close to my cheek. When he attempted to sit down I shot up and looked him in the eyes. He blinked five-six times but didn't look away. His hair was like burnt corn silk, dry and unruly. I smiled and ruffled it. His body lost every trace of stiffness and he gave me an ear-to-ear smile. He had such a wide smile I could see all his molars and even the mouth cavity. We strolled on.

Downtown looked different from those photographs after the 1969 earthquake, which they say brought all kinds of people into the city from the villages round about. President Tito, who loved fondling boys and girls in official photos, came to the city that year to make people forget about the earthquake. My family has a whole book about that, as well as many other Tito books. I wondered how the locals felt after the Presidential party. Probably they had a heavy hangover, even those who didn't drink, because the dog that bit them left no hair behind.

The streets had high curbs and we stumbled over them as we sauntered, silently looking at large windows, tile-less roofs, and the neon letterings above the shops. Many century-old buildings were pressed between the newly built ones with modern shops, like badly done dental work. I couldn't predict what kind of people would come out of these buildings. Men and women were casually dressed, in jeans and shirts, or skirts and blouses. They moved swiftly and purposefully, entering and walking out of stores, some carrying bags, none bothering to look at us, so for a while I felt anonymous, like a strand of grass.

We walked onto a broad street with benches, some bushes, and a couple of birch trees on each side of it. It was overcrowded with young people who looked relaxed. I wondered what they were really like. I felt there was too much work behind that casualness, too much awareness. All the girls had perms, or Tintin tufts sticking up above their foreheads. It was a hairstyle that hadn't reached our town. I didn't much fancy the bushy hair, but soon enough, seeing how they enjoyed their style, constantly correcting the upraised locks, something changed and I started to like it. I pulled my fringe up to make it fountain-like, but it kept falling down.

Aziz said, 'That's pretty.'

'What? Oh no, I'm just, never mind.' I quickly shook my head. My curls quite naturally arranged themselves, especially when my forehead was moist.

As we walked by a group of girls, the word 'peasants' breezed by my ears. We weren't anonymous after all. I knew city people called anyone who didn't live in the centre a peasant, including people in the suburbia. Damn snobs.

Aziz kept stopping and checking street names. I said, 'Are we lost?'

He straightened his back. 'No. It should be, ah there it is.' He strode into a narrow alley and took another couple of turns and we entered an unassuming and dusty little hall with three loose chairs. I stepped up to the dirty glass with a tiny hole at the bottom and peered through it at the man who only heaved a short breath to mark my presence. I didn't really care about registration. I didn't have much sense of or feeling for nationhood, but I didn't want others to make my own decisions, so there I was, disobeying my father. 'I'd like to register.'

'Name and date of birth.'

'Fatima Begovic. Midsummer 1974.'

He shuffled through small cards in a long tin box. 'I already have you here.' He pressed the card against the glass. I could hardly see what all it said. I thought it would say 'Muslim' under nationality but it said 'Yugoslav.' So my father was still a believer in the old brotherhood and unity of nations, which they taught in school until recently.

I said, 'I want to change it.'

He said, with a faint tremor in his voice, 'You pick Serb, Croat, or Muslim.'

'What if I'm a Gypsy? Will I get a nice little badge?' I felt Aziz's hand touch my back and his nervousness flowed into me. I shook it off like a dog would shake off water.

'There's no such nationality.'

I felt so annoyed. I said, 'Put English and change my name to Jane Austen.'

Aziz coughed and the man wiped his right eyebrow. He said, 'Please, make up your mind.'

'I want it to say Bosnian.'

'Will you leave then?'

I nodded and he rewrote my nationality and once again put the paper against the glass. I nodded and plunged out. Aziz came shuffling behind me. For a moment I pitied him. He must have been cursing his damn tongue for even mentioning the wretched registration. It wasn't exactly the most romantic date. I put my head close to Aziz's and smiled. He looked as if he wanted to say he was sorry, but he only smiled a little himself.

We walked around. Aziz looked distressed. Was he afraid? Of what exactly? Then he said, pointing at a bakery before us, 'That's the one.'

'Huh, I'm so hungry. For God's sake, let's eat. Politics is exhausting.'

Aziz chuckled.

The bakery looked like a washed out picture. The paint was peeling off the woodwork. The dimmed glass panes revealed only the foggy shapes of unidentifiable guests. I leaned against the grubby white wooden door. It swung open and I went in.

We sat at one of four aluminium tables that were lined up in a row with four wooden chairs around each. A machine that mixed cool lemonade and a milkish drink called *boza* was hanging from the ceiling, producing an insipid buzz. The whole place had a strained oriental feel. Everything was too overdone in the wrong way: the pictures were too glossy, with old mismatching frames; the ornaments were too deeply carved from the thin tree planks. The waiter with a matchstick in the corner of his mouth came to our table, wiped it clean, dabbed his face with the same cloth and asked what we wanted. He spoke in an indistinguishable accent so he had to gesticulate in confused sign language before we understood what he was offering. Who could say no? Our table became an exhibition of Kosovo dessert cuisine: baklava with thin crispy leaves of dough and a thick layer of walnuts, oozing citrus and honey; ruzica pastry, which looked like small roses with lots of nuts and drenched in sweet, citrus water; three kinds of creamy cakes, one of which had six layers of fruity pudding. I was taking my time with a chocolate-coated, pyramid shaped wafer.

I said playfully, 'The baklava's not anywhere near as good as my mother's.'

Aziz said, after a long delay, 'These long ones, with cream and chocolate, are almost too sweet, but not as sweet as you.'

I twirled my fork in the cream. 'You won't have me blushing.'

He bit his lip and smiled. Then he sighed and patted his stomach to show he couldn't have another one even if his life depended on it. 'It's quite nice around here but I prefer our *mahala*, our neighbourhood.'

'Sure.'

I licked my spoon and murmured, 'So, are we a real couple now, or what?'

Aziz nodded and smiled. He fastened his eyes on the rest of the cake on my saucer, rolling the tip of his tongue around his mouth. I leaned towards him. I was at a breath's distance. He scratched the corner of his right eye and looked at me, his left hand firmly holding the side of the table. He leaned forward, fighting not to close his eyes. I could smell the citrus crispness on his lips. I moved back and said, 'Not here.' He took another bite of cake. I did the same.

He bowed his head and quickly cut the diamond shaped baklava in three, then he pushed it aside. He winked to the waiter, who came with the bill. When Aziz pulled out the president from his wallet and put it on the table, I gently stuck my fork into his hand and slowly pulled it to his fingertips. He smiled without looking at me, and gave the waiter the money.

We left the café and walked to meet the others at the rendezvous place, the bridge close to Kastel ruins. I burnt to know about what Aziz had against Damir. I said, 'You looked like you hated that Damir.'

'My friend Amila used to hang out with him. He means trouble.'

'He looked nice.'

'Trust me, I got to know him in the army. He puts on his damn charms and thinks he owns the world.'

'I see, you're jealous he was hitting on me.'

Aziz exhaled. 'Yes, you're right.'

'That's okay. I kind of like it.'

'You do?'

'Right now I do.'

I put my right hand into his pocket and said, 'I'm cold.'

He blushed and smiled nervously. Back in our town I'd be checking who could see us, who might tell my parents or spread rumours, but here I was so relaxed. Then I saw Elvis leering and pulled back my hand.

A week later Mum found out about the trip. She was as angry as a cartoon character with steam blowing out of her ears; only it was the cold that made her breath visible. 'I won't have you going out with that lad anymore. He's an illiterate peasant and has no prospects.'

'No, he's not. He's smart. You're illiterate yourself.'

Mum slapped me across the eyes with the back of her hand, her ruby ring on her long finger scratching my cheek. I froze, thinking come what may. She screeched, 'I'm a good woman. We paid a lot for your education, a lot. Not even the school library has so many books.'

Yeah, but you can't even read those, I wanted to shout but a surprising flow of tears trickled over my mouth. I wished I knew what made her that way. What made the heat inside her feel cold to me? She went on embroidering her angry speech, 'Your bloke's deranged. Did you know that? Of course you didn't. That's what mothers are for, to help their daughters before they get into trouble and ruin their lives.' Here she hesitated, then went on, 'And you don't need that, take my word for it. Think of poor Nisveta and that man of hers. Deaf as a wall. Think about that.'

She paused, as if to recall what else she could bring up against Aziz. She couldn't look me in the eyes, and she knew she couldn't wait too long for inspiration, so she said briskly, 'This ends here and now. You're lucky I won't tell your father.'

I thought, As if he cared. He hardly talked to us in those days, instead chasing some new carpentry dream, building a new shed, and buying tools. God only knew what that was about. Maybe he couldn't stand Mum's coldness either. When he came inside for lunch, we were still waiting for him. Since Mum was like a fish on land, her mouth opening and shutting, I jumped up and kissed his face, until his tiredness seemed to vanish. I whispered a few words to him and he smiled, looking at Mum. 'I'm hungry,' he said, and went straight to the kitchen, not waiting for a reply.

Other people warned my about Aziz too. I had no idea what everybody was talking about. Nobody seemed to like him and yet everybody liked him well enough when they needed help. People were nice to him when he worked like a horse in their fields. Still, they called him a freak. The secret was damn chaffing. What the hell were they talking about?

One night I couldn't sleep. I was thinking about him. I'd forgotten about Mum and her slap. Twin crescent moons moved across the sky like tipsy women. I was silent. It was chilly and I couldn't see the black sky for all the silent stars, falling or still. The light reflected off the frozen grass. I leaned on the windowpane. It was hard and unnerving, yet good, for it kept my body as tense as my mind. Then Mum came into the room without the slightest noise. I almost jumped on her when she said, 'Beautiful twin moons.'

'You can see those too?' I sagged down under the window.

Mum sank down and sat beside me, as if we were the same body at that midnight hour. She began without hesitation. 'I have to tell you something. I don't want to, but you must know. I don't hate you.'

I peered at the silvery line of her eyelids. Without heaving a breath, she said, 'I didn't want to have daughters, even though imam Atif said daughters were the greatest blessing. They give life even as they are being born.' She glanced at me, and looked quickly away. 'You didn't. It was strange God made it happen that way. But more than anyone, I blame myself. I waited too long to marry and my father desired to have an heir, to leave everything to a grandson and not to the state. I hated all the local men. Once my aunt from eastern Bosnia visited us with her son. He was so handsome and I could feel he was the best man in the world. We loved each other from the first moment. They stayed with us a month. One day our parents found us kissing in the shed, and my father beat Rasim up.'

When she said father's name I could no longer feel my body.

'They left the same evening, but it was already too late.'

I thought my eyes would pop out with staring at her so much. I thought, Too late? Please God don't let it be what I think it is.

'My father wanted to kill me but he died himself, some two months later. My aunt couldn't stop Rasim from coming to me, but she cut all ties. She said we couldn't afford to start a life with scandals and since no one knew Rasim was a relative, it was safe to live here.'

My eyes turned to water. My head fell in her lap and she pressed my eyes with her thumbs and pressed the tears out. I could see again but kept my eyes closed anyway.

'I feared the worse, that you'd be degenerate. I didn't go to hospital. I wanted to do it on my own. I failed and I killed your brother.' She tugged at her brows, and then blew her nose like a trumpet. 'Your father was out of town to buy a new sink. I was such a fool. I ran up and down the hillock behind the house to make the contractions come faster. Once the pains started, I fell in the high grass just outside this room. I fought and fought and you two got tangled. Rasim found me unconscious late that evening and took me to hospital. When they first brought you to me, you were so beautiful. But your brother was dead. I was so glad to have you, even when they told me the boy was dead. Then guilt stuck me like a hammer. I thought God punished me. I stopped loving your father.'

Just as she came to me, silent like a warm wind, she rose and left the room. I went after her and found her in her bed, snoring. I thought she was pretending, so I went close to her and her snores seemed genuine. Over the next few days, she showed no awareness of that night. Maybe she caught herself off guard and wouldn't admit to it. Maybe I was just plain crazy. From that night, she never said anything bad about Aziz. That didn't make it easier for me. For a month I couldn't look my father in the eyes. He'd come into my room when he thought I was asleep and kiss me, sometimes saying, 'Sorry Fatima, for what we've done to you.'

Simple Twist of Fate
(Winter 1991-92)

My mother's confession was such a relief. I knew now what made her the way she was, what made her marriage so strange. Whether or not they loved each other, they still loved me. I inherited my parent's susceptibility for trouble.

One December morning, I woke up with an urge to see Aziz that didn't go away with the cold shower. I was sick and tired of leaving secret messages in a hole under the Rainbow Bridge as to where we could meet. I went straight to him. Aziz's street was a little alley, with a row of slender birch trees on both sides, heavy with snow. His house was close to the pavement, as if built so to make it easier to watch passers-by. There was no fence facing the street; only on the sides separating their property from their neighbours.

I walked buoyantly over the unfamiliar gravel of his backyard. Aziz gawked at me and clenched his teeth. His parents gazed at me, waiting for the courtesy of inquiring about their health. Aziz was sitting in a kind of shed without walls, just a simple roof on four pillars. He had a pile of husked corn at his feet, and was holding an uncapped bottle of water. I looked up. The sun was weak and the light milky. Something was missing. Grapevines. A backyard with no grapevines had a feel of poverty even on a winter day. I associated it with never-relaxed muscles, unnecessary sweat, and confinement to the coolness of the house on hot days.

Aziz's toes curled. He plunged towards me, stumbling over the tools scattered around a pile of chopped wood. I shuddered as his ankle barely missed the axe leaning against a large log. He stopped mere inches from me, but I didn't step towards him.

'*Salaam alaykum*. How are you?' I said to his parents with a courtly smile. Aziz stood beside me, mute. I didn't look at him.

'*Wa alaykum-u-salaam.* Very well, thank you. How're your parents?'

'They're fine. They send their regards.'

They took their time staring at me before his Mum said, 'You tell them we'd like them to come and visit us sometime.'

'I will, thank you.'

'It's so warm today.' Aziz's Mum wiped her forehead with her apron. I suspected she was suffering like Mum: becoming old, losing her period, her body going from normal to hot then to freezing in a matter of seconds. She was a hefty woman and the sweat dribbled much more profusely than my own Mum's. Two thin braids fell from her loosely tied scarf, which had worn embroidery along the edges that time had tattered away. She turned towards her husband, a tall and lean man with a sunburnt face and prominent cheekbones. 'Ibrahim, it's so hot. I'll make us some cold lemonade. Would you children like some?'

Ibrahim zipped his winter jacket. He had a big, intoxicating smile. His powerful voice didn't seem to come from that emaciated body. 'Of course they would Behara; they're not ill.'

Typical of Bosnian men to protest against such questions. Refreshments and sweets were supposed to be presented to guests, and it was left to them whether or not they wanted any.

I smiled back. 'Oh, I'm fine, thank you. I'm not thirsty and I can't stay long.'

'I'll be right back with the glasses.'

Behara winked at Ibrahim and they both disappeared behind the closing door.

Aziz breathed out as if he had been holding his breath all along. He almost hissed, 'You can't just call on me like this.'

I screwed up my eyes. 'I can hardly hear you. Why are you whispering?'

'Why are you here? You know what people will say.'

'I couldn't care less.'

'But it's you I'm thinking of.'

'Maybe you're more afraid of what people will say about you.'

He gulped. 'You're right.'

'Sure I am.'

'I love it when you're tough.'

'Liar.' I smiled.

He guffawed. 'You're incredible. Come, I'll show you something. I live up there.'

'In the attic? Really? You never tell me anything.'

'It's not finished yet, but come, I'll show you.'

I eyed the yard and the house. It looked rather desolate. When I heard the front door open and glasses clinking, I pushed Aziz inside and closed his door. Despite my brazen attitude, I asked, 'What about your parents?'

'Don't worry.' He went down to fetch the lemonade. I ambled around, without Aziz's breath following an inch from my neck. I already liked the warmth. I checked the first two doors to the toilet and the kitchen, then walked straight into the oblong lounge. Dust was the third presence in the room, coiling around the thick beams of light from the large window. I rubbed the tip of my nose. The room had the cloying smell of sweat and clammy cologne. The opposite of my house. I loved it.

Aziz came back short of breath, carrying a tray of biscuits and two brimming glasses. I sat down on the sofa under the window, turning my head around as if there was more to see. 'Nice,' I said through my pursed lips and looked at the other sofa on the opposite side.

Aziz put the tray on the table in the middle. 'I got the sofas in exchange for the junk Father used to keep here.'

'My father's the same; he doesn't use half the tools he's filled the shed with.'

Aziz pointed at the small round window above me. 'You can see the street from here. But people can't see you.'

'Good. And the TV fits perfectly over there. You can lie on either sofa and see it just fine. Does it work?'

'Sure, why?' He put his lower lip over his upper, and it looked as if he was pulling his face down. His nostrils opened wide.

'It's almost five and Beverly Hills 90210 is on.'

'I've never seen it. Is it good?' He turned on the TV.

'It's okay. I like this bloke Dylan. He's rather cute.'

'I don't watch much TV.'

'There, it's starting. They show all the characters first. You see that blond bloke and that brunette? They're twins, only they don't look anything like each other. Oh, there's Dylan. He always comes last. He's kind of important. I like his eyebrows.'

Aziz stroked his own brows and said, 'You should come here to watch every episode.'

'That'd be great. Hush now!'

An hour later, the room contracted to the rhythm of the sighs that we were hopelessly trying to hide from one another. Aziz turned off the TV and turned on the radio. I wanted him to grab me and pull me over to his sofa. He was calm as a painting. The radio was tuned to a foreign station. I listened to the lyrics, sang by a terrible male voice; something about a meeting in a park at evening a twist of fate.

Aziz opened the window and another tune from a party somewhere down the street swept into the room. The sound of a distant accordion somehow made me lose strength. I couldn't lift my arms or move my feet.

'Somebody's going to do his military service soon,' Aziz said, and shuddered.

'What's on your mind?'

'The only good thing about the army was the looks of girls along the roads when we marched to the shooting range. Beans and hard bread, comradeship and discipline are overrated. I was a hard-working lad already. The army didn't make me a man.' He looked across the room, as if looking for something. 'The other blokes didn't like me much. I wasn't slick or amusing. I couldn't play any instrument and I hated gambling. I didn't get drunk on weekends or leave my post to meet with girls.'

'I guess I'll never have to experience that.'

'That poor bloke down there will probably be sent off to Croatia to kill people there. Things are getting bad.'

'I don't know much about it. I never watch news. And I don't think anything will happen here in Bosnia.'

'That's not what I've heard. People are gloomy these days, don't you think? I don't want to be a soldier and kill people for no reason, or for any damn reason.' He glanced at me. 'What would you think of me in a uniform?'

'You'd look handsome, tough and elegant, important. Soldiers look important.'

He buried his chin in his chest and leaned closer. My fingers itched. He said, 'In the service, a couple of blokes tied me to a tree and left me there the whole night with my penis hanging out of my trousers. They said they wanted to see if I could piss like a man, not sitting down on the toilet.'

'What? Incredible. So you take a leak sitting, so what? So does my father. Except when we're out in the field and he just does it standing behind a tree or something. That Damir we met in the city. Was he one of them?'

'No, but he stood aside watching, and he didn't go to the lieutenant to report it.'

'Arsehole.' I nudged him with my elbow and we both peered through the window. The future soldier danced with every girl who was keen for a swing. His father broke a plate with his palm when a tune hit a nerve in his heart. The sober and sobbing mother, who was otherwise constantly fetching more refreshments for the happy crowd, smashed one herself.

The musician with the accordion stretched his arms wide, as if to embrace the lad with it. The openings in his instrument were full of money. The father came close to the violin player and put money between the strings, which then sounded more cheerful.

I stroked Aziz's hip. He took me by the shoulders and we kissed as if we didn't know breathing was allowed. I mounted him, afraid to pull my lips back. There were no tactics, no plan. I wanted to conquer him at any price and with no hesitation, with no second thoughts. His trousers didn't bulge immediately, as I'd expected. I rubbed myself against his thigh, and his hands roamed all over me. At last, I felt his penis hardening. He lifted me up a couple of times to stop himself. I pressed my body down, again and again. And again. He didn't try to take my wet trousers off, nor would he let me unbutton his. Our breathing became harsh, my breath pushing into his mouth and his breath rushing into mine. I fainted. I think I did.

I woke up in the middle of the following night, dressed as when I was with Aziz. I thought I must have dreamt everything. The room was bare. I didn't see him anywhere. But I could smell him on my fingers, my clothes. I pushed the windows open, and felt emptiness inside. I couldn't fall asleep again until sunrise.

Beverly Hills 90210 ceased at the beginning of spring 1992. It was a damn stupid show anyway. Aziz and I met at least a couple of times a week. Mostly making out, except he still wouldn't let me touch him. I was so frustrated I didn't notice I no longer had nails to nibble. He neglected the farm and his duties. His brother Weasel spread the rumour that Ibrahim once found him on the floor having a catnap. Normally, Aziz would be the first to get up in the mornings and the last to go to bed. I didn't pay much attention to the rumours. I figured they were jealous that a bloke like him could ignore all those who'd been using him and instead give more time to me, or thinking about me. I loved that, being the grand prize in somebody's life. But the damn secret was killing me.

Secret
(Spring 1992)

Close to the beginning of the fasting month, Ramadan, I decided to find out what this was all about. If there was a secret with Aziz's crotch, I needed to know. I walked into Aziz's room like a toddler, testing the ground. I looked at everything but him, and said, 'The TV's off.'

He shrugged his shoulders. After a while he said, 'It's broken.'

'I see.'

'Why don't you sit down?'

'I have to go.'

He stood up. 'Stay.'

I came closer and let him kiss me. I said, 'Whatever it is, I want to know.'

He held his upper lip tight against his teeth. He smelled like overripe tomatoes. I waited him out. His face twitched a couple of times and for a moment he looked away. I thought I'd exhausted the possibilities, trying to make sense of him in all the ways I possibly could, but it was only when he let my hands open his trousers and pull them down that I realised how feeble my imagination really had been, how wrong I'd been interpreting every damn little move he'd made. I'd had no idea of how brave he was to trust me.

There was nothing strange with his penis. Not that I had seen many before. It was long, thick, and circumcised. Milky fluid was dripping from it. I didn't lift up my head to give him a smile of relief. I didn't want him to get it all wrong, whatever that was. I took it with both my hands and still the reddish tip hung outside my fists. He didn't moan, or react in any way. Then I felt the secret, and knew there was no turning back. I dropped on the floor and put my head right under his crotch.

He was a freak. He had a vagina, right under his member. I had no idea what he could do with it, whether he could have children or... I was even afraid to think of the possibilities. And it was there. It was a fact, incredible like summer hail, but undeniable. I felt the cut. It was just as long as my own. The sides of it like thick petals just about to bud.

My lips were two glued pebbles, but my brain was a pool with more eels than water in it. I don't know how long I knelt there, staring at it, my nails buried in his thighs. I heard rapid whispers, 'Forgive me forgive me forgive me forgive me.'

I grabbed his prick, but it had turned like dough. I stood up, wiped my palms against his face.

I left.

I didn't rush back home. I dragged my feet over the familiar gravel. My arms and head itched deep under the skin and muscles, right in the bones. I took handfuls of hair and tugged at the locks. Long, blond hairs fell down onto my crumpled, pink blouse. I tucked the blouse into my trousers. I kneeled at the creek just below my house. The sprucing water pricked me back from the feeling of being in a dream. I took time looking at my palms, questioning my eyes, the tactility of my fingers. I even doubted my nose, for it sensed a familiar smell down there.

Why was I so disappointed? I'd wanted him on his back. My god, and he never even mentioned anything, not once. Fear, I guess. Yet damn bold he was all along. Damn bold. Something like that and he dared to keep dating me, kissing me, constantly having in mind everything that could go wrong.

I didn't wash my hands, arms, mouth, cheeks, or eyes. I dragged myself home, wondering if he was a woman nipped in the bud. I almost managed to smile at the way my imagination was working. I was amazed at his audacity. The cheek. We'd been dating for so long. Was I so blind to the signs? Perhaps he was constantly making himself forget about it. Perhaps his love enabled him to ignore it and hope for the best. Perhaps he was just desperate and…

The following day was Ramadan. Custom was to have longer evening prayers called *teravih*. I persuaded Mum to come with me, even though she no longer cared about prayers. Father, he couldn't care less about anything. He was constantly working, as usual. Why did I want to go? I have no idea. Maybe I was hoping to see Aziz as much as I burnt to avoid him.

Trickle after trickle of the locals welled out of alleys, flowing down the main street, exchanging surreptitious glances covered by semi-darkness, and neighbourly comfort. That Ramadan, people talked about horrible things happening in other parts of Yugoslavia. Minaret lights in Bosnia were suddenly more than signs for fasting people to let the tools fall and the cutlery clink against earthenware dishes. The electric candles now attracted swarms of bullets. The local mosque was only twenty years old and didn't have as many inscriptions, ornaments, carvings, and paintings on the walls as the centuries-old Turkish ones in Banja Luka. The top of its slender minaret was lined with light bulbs called *kandilj*, which the imam turned on at the first trace of evening, when it was time for *iftar*, dinner. The floor was covered with an oriental wall-to-wall carpet. Its wool was soft and warm in cold winters, but cool in spring or summer.

I sat on the balcony. I moved back from the rim to avoid scouring the throng of men for a glimpse of Aziz. I heard the entrance door creak and looked down. Aziz barged into the mosque late the first evening. I put my nose through the fence, and out of an odd instinct I almost cried, 'Hey you, climb up here!' He sat down in a corner. The mosque was not crowded to bursting point, but the air was hot and the walls were sweaty. I liked that everybody was talking at the same time. The chatter flooded my mind and I didn't have to think of Aziz. I peered down again and met his tearful eyes. Neither of us blinked until the muezzin's recitation brought silence. I moved back to sit in a straight line with the other women. Mum tugged my skirt from behind to make me move closer to her, but I pulled it back.

Imam Atif rose from the assembly, slowly walked up a little stair to his left, and knit his hands over his bulky stomach. He had a white cape and a fez wrapped with a white cloth, He spoke softly, 'Sisters and brothers.' His eyes were saggy in the corners, like his shoulders. I consumed his calm. His old voice echoed, 'Yet another Ramadan has come to embellish our days with innumerable gifts.'

I hoped his speech would make me stop thinking about Aziz, and it did, for a short while. It was brief and I felt as if he was speaking directly to me, as if he knew my pains. 'Erudite people say fasting is a tool given by the Benevolent to provoke empathy, encourage giving, and harness our hatred. Even wicked tongues have difficulty rolling when mouths are sticky with thirst. It makes us remember those who don't have their daily bread, as Christians say, or those who are different. I, on the other hand, don't think we become merciful because of hunger, but in spite of it. Whoever survived the big war, knows what I'm talking about. Hunger, thirst, and pain make us focus on ourselves. We step on other souls for a scoopful of lukewarm water.'

He wiped his mouth and finished, 'It's in spite of hunger, thirst, or pain that we think of our common good. Ramadan teaches us not to forget how to be good. If anything evil happens in Bosnia, remember this.'

He described me, I thought. I was in pain and that made me selfish. I only feared what troubles Aziz's deformity was going to cause me. The Imam warned me against myself.

Unaffected by the sweat running down his face, the imam looked over the people and gave a sign to the muezzin to begin his part. The prayer was long, too long. I couldn't concentrate. I could no longer hear recitations. Still, I kept falling down on my forehead at the right moments, my body following the rhythm of the women around me. Once the movements stopped, I opened my eyes. Everybody had left. Mum was not there either, but shortly she turned up at the door and cried, 'Well come on, Fatima. What are you waiting for?'

'I'll be right there.' I looked over the fence. Aziz sat alone under the strong lights of an enormous chandelier, like a dream-catcher, only with hundreds of crystal balls tied with brass threads. He looked at the balcony, still tearful. He pinched his thighs with all his fingers. I couldn't bear to look at his sweet puppy eyes, so I darted out.

I was still freaked out. What a damn interesting word, freaked out by a freak of nature, or perhaps it was a divine gift. I didn't know where to begin to look. Not in my old biology schoolbooks for sure. I had no idea what that deformity was called, what caused it, if it existed anywhere else, in any other time. If it did, someone sure must have recorded it. I liked to read fiction, but the shock made me check the facts.

I found nothing. Not one single thing. For the best, I thought. Did I need a book to tell me what to think about Aziz? I could make up my own damn mind. Maybe there weren't any others like him; he was unique and he was mine. But still what could I do to stop thinking of him as a freak?

Two weeks later my eyes had fasted more than my belly: not a proper look at Aziz for days. How could that be in such a small town? As the days went by I missed him terribly, I found that I did not care about what I'd seen that day in his garret. Mum was content with the situation. Whenever we went to the mosque, she kept tight by my side. She dressed up in a black skirt, and a gold-embroidered blouse. She smelled of some bitter desert musk someone told her was the latest fashion in Mecca. I wore mostly thin cardigans over a T-shirt and a skirt.

Every evening, on the way back from the mosque, I hummed Aziz's song, silently in the broken darkness of my room, hearing the ticking of the clocks, imagining Aziz hidden behind the waterfalls, under the Rainbow Bridge, and having a little peek at his bait. Should I wait for another twist of fate?

The twenty-seventh night of Ramadan, the time when God promised to be more susceptible to all the prayers crowding before him, really turned out blessed more than a thousand months. My prayer was granted.

The air was heavy on my shoulders and I could hardly breathe. A silence hung in the night that was almost tangible. I could hear no nervous sighs of swarming insects, nor any night birds on watch. An owl flew silently from tree to tree then dived like quicksilver towards the dark brook where I'd almost rinsed my nose of Aziz's smell. The air stood still in the parched blackness of the tree crowns.

Then, as if at a genuine intruder, our bitch barked. I winced and heard a window open and my sleepy father yelled 'Shut up' at the dog. I opened my window just as a pebble hit the wall an inch beneath the glass. I called out, 'Are you trying to kill me?' Then I smiled at Aziz. He leaned on the house, panting. He said, 'No no no. But you opened it right when I threw the stone. You're reading my mind?'

'Always. Where the hell have you been all this time?'

'I don't know. Around and about.'

'You have no excuse. I didn't even have a curfew. My parents just told me to be cautious and that they didn't want to pry into my choices.'

Aziz fell silent for a moment then said, 'I'm sorry for what I did.'

'No need. I don't care.'

'You don't?'

'I mean I care about you, you silly thing.'

'Then you have to hear me out.' He put his chin against the house and I protruded my head out of the window and put my chin against the wall in the same way.

'You don't have to say anything, Aziz.' I didn't want to push him. I didn't want to hurt him, really. As much as I was dying to find out at least a little, I didn't want to hear any explanations.

'I must.' It took a lot of fidgeting, sighing, and scratching his neck and stomach before he began, 'I was lucky…that Mum decided I was a boy. I still have nightmares of wearing women's clothing half my life then switching to a bloke's, or the other way round.' He was clear and calm; he must have been mulling over this little speech for a while. 'I don't know what I am, Fatima. In school, no one ever taught us about such things. I don't know if there's a name for it. I only know what Mother told me, that it isn't normal, that it isn't okay.' I wished he'd look me in the eyes, but he kept peering at the wall. 'I've always been a boy, but…'

I said, 'Do you use it?' I could have slapped myself, what did I mean by 'use it,' what stupid question was that?

He was still calm. 'I know you have a million questions but I just can't answer them. I really don't know much myself, I don't know what it means if stuff is running from it, or that I pee with only my… Please, I beg you, don't try to touch me there.' He rubbed his forehead against the façade.

'Don't do it! I feel bad when you do that.'

He went silent and slouched by the wall. After a few minutes I whispered, 'Maybe you should come in. I have a free spot over here.'

'I'm coming.' He made for the wall, looking for openings in the brick façade that were big enough for his fingers. There were none. The house was still like new and the cement between the bricks was practically untouched.

'No, you silly creature. You can't.'

'But you said.'

'I was just thinking out loud. I'm not sure we should test my parents too much.'

He flustered. 'I have to kiss you.'

'Here.' I kissed my fingertips and waved.

'Come out.'

'All right. Just one quick peck.'

He ran around the house and stood by the front door. The bitch didn't give a peep. She liked him too. I opened the front door but didn't turn on the lights. I moved towards Aziz's breath, which smelled like dry saliva, and found two hands stretched out to lead me. Aziz's hands were wet and he dried them against his trousers beneath the knees. I felt like a prim, well-bred country girl, proud as a duchess and blushing like a dairymaid, opening the door to my beloved and seeing him standing there on the dark threshold, shy and handsome. I was next to him and he bent over me, taking my head between his palms.

We went to the shed. I was so damn curious. I wanted to explore him between the legs. He trembled when I kneeled and tried to take him in my mouth. He swept a bunch of tools off Father's waist-high working table, lifted me from the ground like a cup, and put me on the table. I only wore my negligee. The cold metal edges felt so good against my hot skin, like when you eat salty peanuts with melted chocolate, opposite in nature but mixed together they give a whole new sensation.

I hitched out his belt from his trousers, which then fell down around his feet. I lay on my back. He climbed on the table and mounted me. When he entered me, it felt it like a short, sharp cut. A rivulet of lukewarm fluid ran down my thigh. The lingering pain rippled to the edges of my body, cuddling me.

Then the damn river took an unexpected turn again. On Bayram 1992, the festivity at the end of Ramadan, I found Aziz buying sugar at Ibro's kiosk, which was a small, wooden shed, rather than a real kiosk. I came running to Aziz. My face was swollen like an overripe plum, wet with tears, and smeared with dust. Aziz shot up like a jump-started car. 'My God, what happened?' He was already hugging me and removing tangled locks from my eyes.

I sobbed. 'I was in a fight!'

'Fight?'

'That fat cow Milena beat me with her bag.'

'Why?'

'She and some other Serb girls teased me for being in school at Bayram, said they'd never be there on Christmas or Easter. Then they boasted about their brothers joining the Yugoslav Army and all that shit and I told them to go home and fuck with their Chetnik brothers. They jumped me and I hit my head on the corridor bench.'

He felt the back of my head with his fingertips and gave me a hug. 'It'll be all right.'

I pushed him. 'No it won't! Come with me! You must punish them!'

'What are you saying? I can't punish them.'

'You must show them they can't do that! You make them look like this!' I pointed to my face.

'I can't beat up girls.'

'You arsehole! You have to do something!' I grabbed his hand, but he pulled me back and made me sit down under the kiosk. The ninety-year-old Ibro mumbled short prayers against evil spirits.

'I can't, Fatima. Sorry. I can't beat up those girls. We should talk.'

'You freak!' I screamed like a crow. 'You chicken heart. I thought you loved me.' I smacked him across his sandpapery chin and ran off. I spent the rest of the day shunning my family. I couldn't let them know what had happened. Mum was the difficult one, of course, but when I told her through the locked door that I'd help her starch and iron all those brocades and her other old silly stuff, she gave up trying to come into my room. The next morning, I woke up two hours earlier than usual. I looked better, but the anger was like a windmill. I took handfuls of stones, and went to wait for the bullies to pass Yellow Bridge, which they always did. Out of a dozen, only two pebbles missed the targets.

I didn't go to school that day. I loitered on the bank, flipping pebbles over the surface. In the afternoon, on the way home, a boy in tatters ran towards me like a blind chicken, kicking a ball. He glided in between my legs as if he was trying to tackle me. He was lying there at my feet, peering at me with a pair of big bright eyes through his long, ruffled hair. He couldn't stop panting and staring at me. Then he said, 'The war has begun.'

The News
(Spring – Autumn 1992)

Bayram fell on the 2nd of April 1992. It was a time for festivities, kids walking from door to door congratulating the adults and getting sweets or small change. That Bayram was feast-less. Nobody knocked on our door. People were watching news.

The usual newscaster Senad Hadzifejzovic commenced with a hint of insecurity beneath the calm surface of professionalism. Mum wrung her hands. Although her pale knuckles didn't make a sound, Father grabbed both of her hands with his one fist. The knuckles crackled under his pressure, and when he released them, she dropped her hands to her knees like icicles.

At first, I didn't shiver in the cold air of my house, get goose bumps, or start cold-sweating. My hair didn't rise and my mouth was still fresh and full of saliva. Then my imagination flared like some old injury. I imagined myself sitting behind Senad's wide white desk. The dull glass of a camera was six feet away, yet felt as if pressed against my face, my eyelashes brushing the glass. Then I realised newsmen should never blink. I imagined myself preparing to face the world. I screamed in my head, How's the news to be conveyed? Who's listening? For what reasons? What about the aggressors? Is there a rocket breaking the outer wall of the building? Will it make its way to Studio C where the whole thing's being recorded?

A voice sounded, 'Three, two, one, you're on.' My thought was cut short, and I was back in my house. Senad heaved a short breath announcing:

'It's not official. It hasn't been declared, but it's already fair to say: This is war. War against the innocent. War against our children. War against all of us. 'We are not killing each other. The Serbs are killing us. Don't listen to rumours. Don't believe anything you've not seen for yourself. This is a war waged with special means, not limited to mere arms. Now we have the absolute right to ask: where is the government we voted for in our first free and democratic election? Where are the deputies? I am anxious to call them back to their parliamentary benches. Yet I fear this war is the result of their vile language. We wouldn't exaggerate if we claimed that the last bastion of common sense and brotherhood is the media: RTV Sarajevo, Oslobodenje, and YUTEL.'

Senad took a short break and I had time to check on my family. They were still stiff and mute. I wanted to hear their comments, but before I managed to open my lips to ask, Senad went on, 'You can hear the reactions of the editors-in-chief of these media.' Then, one after the other, news announcers from different TV and radio channels weighed in with their comments.

From that day on, I didn't miss any piece of news I could get when there was no power cut, or when we had enough batteries for the radio. I only knew about the events in Sarajevo, Gorazde, Srebrenica, Mostar, Bihac, and other places from the TV. I guess that's not much more than what any other news junky in the world got his kicks from. Maybe army generals and the authorities had more insight into the progress of warfare, but simple people certainly didn't. If ever TV or radio news communicated the full scope of war, it still came to me only in fragments. Even when I was in the middle of it, I knew only what was immediate to me. Everything else was rumour.

I never really understood what the whole conflict was about, how it all started, and who won in the end. The whole truth will probably never end up in the hands of ordinary drudges. There were so many nationalities in the Balkans. In Bosnia, people of traditionally orthodox faith were called Serbs because they saw themselves as belonging to Serbia; people of Catholic faith called themselves Croats for the same reason. There were Muslims all over former

Yugoslavia but only the ones in Bosnia called themselves Boshniaks or just plain Bosnians because being a Muslim wasn't really a nationality. A veritable Balkan casserole, and I never found out if all the Bosnian Gypsies and Jews called themselves Bosnians or something else. Everybody suddenly hated everybody. Yugoslavia was falling apart into the bunch of small countries that had formed the Yugoslav union after the Second World War. The Serbs, led by Milosevic, attacked every Republic that wanted independence. Eventually, the Balkan peoples were killing each other. The Serbs tried to rid themselves of the Croats, but eventually both of these wanted to take a piece of Bosnia, the country in-between theirs. That's why we Bosnians call the war an aggression on Bosnia and not a civil war. Bosnians never attacked anyone outside the Republic's legitimate borders.

Bosnia was a small country, but war had different faces in different parts of it. Every place, every man woman child had a different story to tell, yet they were all old damn clichés that any immigration judge was fed up with hearing after the first few asylum cases.

I knew from the news that the Serbs were demolishing Sarajevo, the capital. They didn't care who was in the streets when they shelled and torched. They killed even those Serbs who opposed the aggression. A damn mess. They didn't shell my town. I don't know why. War strategies are out of my grasp. My father once said they saved us like good wine and cheese; something they could come to after hard work elsewhere, a dessert. I don't know about that.

Love: what happened with that trump card? Love conquers all, and all that jazz. The war brought us together as a family for the first time in years. We sat tight like dumb fish, staring at the screen. I don't really remember every piece of news but some of the scenes are like cigarette burns on my brain, especially the first. No one ever forgets the first time. I tried to recall everything so I would never forget it. It wasn't easy.

*

In the first months of the war, there were no fights in our town. We couldn't always watch the news, because the power cuts started almost immediately. The Serbs downsized Sarajevo to its graveyards and yet not even those were left untouched, as if the aggressors also had unspeakable hatred of the dead. Before I knew it, it was April 5th. I don't even recall what happened in the three days after the first news. Did we turn into thoughtless zombies in between the news?

The opening music for the news was different, more bombastic with trumpet and trombone tones. Senad showed the footage of the massacre of protesters against the war at some place called Vrbanja Bridge, a recreation spot. A reporter from TV Sarajevo recorded the words of a local artist, Alma Suljevic, who was demonstrating at Vrbanja. This woman raged, 'I'd just like the camera to film my bloody hand! So far, this hand has only made sculptures for this city. Now there's blood on them, the blood of a girl the Serbs killed. We were standing on this bridge demonstrating against the aggression and they answered by discharging a volley at us, as if we weren't people, as if we weren't living beings.'

I'd never seen that woman before, but she felt like a sister.

Mum sat behind Father and tied her arms around his chest sobbing and whispering, 'Soon it'll be our turn, soon it'll be our turn.'

Later on and, as if only artists had things to say, Senad announced, 'The control room informs me that our eminent fellow citizen, Emir Kusturica, now in Paris, is on the line now.'

Kusturica, the guru of Balkan cinema, our most beloved filmmaker wasn't in the country; he never experienced the war but was somewhere abroad, safe, throwing comments, 'I'm upset… However, if we glance back at that which preceded today's experience of these wretched people, we can easily conclude that all of it was their own choice! The people chose their own misfortunes.'

Father jumped up and circled in the room. He stomped to the TV and attempted to shut it down, but he ended up listening instead. Kusturica went on, 'I doubt a personal effort can bring about much... I firmly believe and claim that the Federal Yugoslav Army still has the potential and strength to save the people, in an anti-nepotistic way.'

Father yelled so the windows vibrated, 'Are you out of your damn mind, Emir? What's wrong with you? Everybody knows the Serbs command the Federal Army. They are killing civilians. Who else has tanks and fighter jets?'

Days burned up like New Year fireworks. Father wouldn't let me go outside for a month. I wondered why Aziz didn't come to check on me. Maybe he did come, but didn't dare knock on the door. Maybe he didn't. I missed him, yet couldn't make myself do anything.

On June 8th I missed the evening broadcast but Mum and Father were as usual glued to the screen. I was stuck on the toilet with nasty diarrhoea. I spent an hour and a half walking in and out of the bathroom, like that cartoon character Balthazar used to do when trying to come up with a big-time invention. Mum barged in like a cheerful bird, breathing heavily, not bothered by the smell, and rambled on about something to do with miracles, birth and death, love and whatnot. 'Fatima, listen to this. The news said that last night some incredible woman gave birth to twins, a boy and a girl. Imagine that, with no doctor, with only a midwife present. Senad said, "This country is brimming with love".'

Both twins survived, I thought, but I didn't feel too exalted. Instead, I laughed at Senad's sarcasm, something that became his hallmark. For a while, I felt like I was having an affair with this Senad. He was handsome enough to make me forgive his age, which I guessed was forty-five.

*

The war changed Aziz. It changed everything. But it was him that I cared for. For a moment, the fear that the Serbs would barge into our houses and kill us all made me forget about our shaky relationship and his deformity. I remembered only the good things, the things we saw together, and the smells that affected us differently.

When Aziz came to my house, he first stared at the front door, or through my window. His forehead was sweaty and his always-sunburnt cheeks washed with fresh tears. This spooked my parents. It felt as if he was always there, like a silent guardian. I loved seeing him hunched close to our bitch, nuzzling her between the ears. Animals could never resist Aziz.

I decided to cut through this spell and ignore my parents by going to his place more often. We'd meet and sit silently for hours. Then, as if it were for the last time, we'd kiss madly and make love. I thought we were lucky that I was never knocked up. I never suspected anything else. For three or four months, we hardly exchanged a word. I never asked why he was silent because I understood his silence, it mirrored my own. What could any of us possibly say that would in any way change our situation?

On August 29th I decided I mustn't miss an opportunity to sing a tune. Two birthdays. The first one was announced on the news: Bosnia celebrated its eight hundred and third birthday (it was born in 1189, with Kulin Ban's Charter). The second one was Aziz's, his twenty-sixth. I took a huge candle and stuck it in a half loaf of bread; since there was a shortage of sugar those days it meant no cake. I put the wannabe cake on the bedside table, in the middle of the night. I sometimes slept over at his place; my parents weren't too happy about it but they didn't judge me. I sang the Bosnian version of Happy Birthday, and he just couldn't believe I'd remembered. While I sang, he smiled and rubbed his face, but he anxiously glanced out of the window a couple of times for fear some passing military jeep might stop, as if I my voice was that strong. That night he was aroused like never before. I felt as if he was touching me deep inside.

It took a while before the Serbs worried over what to do with people in my town. Father said, 'They're in majority in our town and rule it politically already. There's no need to kill us off right away when there's resistance in many other places in Bosnia.'

Day as night we watched lorries pass by pass by pass by, with artillery covered by dappled cloths. Serbian soldiers winked to the girls who dared to be in the streets. Sometimes we heard a din from the other side of the mountain, which meant the Serbs were meeting resistance, but we had no idea who was putting it up or how.

On September 10th it smelled as if the summer was still around. It smelled of green tomatoes and of dust rising from the ground after a short shower. The crust beneath the rows of tomato plants was softening and sounded like simmering milk on the stove. The lush vegetables smelled refreshing. It rained and more and more dark clouds billowed from the east. The air was thick with fireflies and cricket-song. The news announced an event called Sefard, four centuries of the expulsion of the Jews from Spain and their arrival in Sarajevo. In Bosnia, both Jews and Muslims shared the same fate.

That day, I turned off the TV. Mum and Father didn't react to the silence. Perhaps I'd read their minds and simply acted on their own wishes. The darkness outside was weak and I stepped towards the window like a sleepwalker. They went to the kitchen, and Mum whispered too loudly, 'We have to do something. We can't wait around to be killed.'

Father answered, whispering as well, 'I wouldn't worry. I think this will stop soon. Nobody's threatened us so far. What can we do anyway?'

'Don't be such a coward,' Mum hissed.

Father ignored her tone. 'I heard Serbian refugees came to Banja Luka from Croatia, and that the offensives in western Bosnia will force the Muslim population to head our way.'

He was right; soon refugees begun to arrive. Their cheeks were simmering in the unusual autumn heat. Their hair was dust-white, grizzled by the days and nights spent in the open. Their cardboard faces were stiff and stony. Their stuff was on tractors, carts, donkeys, and on their own backs. They weren't thin and emaciated, like walking skeletons, for they were just at the beginning of their careers as refugees. Nonetheless, they didn't look like sensible creatures. Even the young looked empty as cartridges. My thoughts were coiling and uncoiling like thin green snakes, gliding around, trying to bite their own tails.

The refugees marched into my town as if there were no dead-ends or cul-de-sacs, as if they'd never stop, unless we pulled them off the road and embraced them. They looked damned to always search for the true meaning of a hearth, of home, even when huddled in warm rooms. But there was something else in their new way of being that I liked, the inescapable closeness of the next man. They were forced to rely upon one other, and keep one another warm.

Except for some old townspeople who'd seen at least one world war and immediately offered their help, the rest of the locals stood motionless along the main street, mutely watching the dusty crowd. The whole sight was like a collective, prophetic dream of our own future. Out of the silence, a local woman at last cried out, 'They are heading for the school!'

Another voice woke up out of the crowd, 'Let's go to Omer at Merhamet. He'll know what to do.'

Someone else said, 'Come on, people! Don't just stand there! It's not polite to stare at people like that! Let's make sure they get what they need!'

The next moment, people rushed in all directions. 'Wait for me!' echoed randomly from several sides as the crowd along the street slowly rippled away, leaving eddies of dust behind them. I thought it was rude to chat, or even worse, to swear and grunt as some people did until their mouths were sticky and they had to shut up so as not to choke on their own tongues. I went back home and rummaged through my closet for any clothes I didn't wear any longer. I practically emptied it, leaving only a few t-shirts, a pair of good Levi 501s, and two sweaters I'd got from Mum as birthday presents. The rest I put in a big black bag and left outside the Merhamet office. I knew the personnel would make sure the clothes ended up in the right hands.

The local families offered shelter to refugees. But no matter how well meaning we were, the name refugee could never be washed from the loosening seams of their clothes.

Mum didn't say a word about refugees. She never suggested that we take care of a family. When Father mentioned the possibility she simply ignored him. I saw Father give money to some broken down men and women when they came to our house asking for help. Mum kept frantically cleaning the house from morning until late in the evening. Either she was nasty, or she was losing her mind. I wanted to tug her hair and shout, 'Wake up for God's sake.' Two days later, when I heard her coming to clean my room, I deliberately opened the door to my closet to see her reaction. At first she was surprised the room was clean, that no clothes were hanging from the ceiling lamp or lay splayed over the floor. She peered into the closet and at the two sole hangers with a sweater on each.

I expected a slap on the head, or at least some shouting. I hated her silence. I wanted her to be strong and alive even if that meant I'd get regular portions of nagging and scolding instead of meals.

She said through a laugh, 'You saved these two I made for you.'

'Of course.'

She ran towards me and kissed me all over the face. I was so drenched in her milk-smelling saliva I needed a towel to wipe it off, but I didn't dry my face. I let the traces of her kisses dry so I could smell them when distant explosions woke me up at night.

One evening, just across the river and into the woods, Aziz and I were talking and exchanging kisses. A blazing cloud skimmed the sky and vanished behind the hill. Even though we were sitting next to each other, I tried to move closer to him, as if my part of the bench was too cold and his part had all the warmth. He held a single, sun-coloured primrose. He twisted off its top and used its stalk to make sounds like a small, squeaking trumpet, to make me laugh. It was a windless, uncannily smell-less afternoon.

I felt somebody was watching us. I turned and squinted, looking at the familiar figure of a man standing behind the rusty fence of a little house. Just a few months ago, the fence was overgrown with wild rose bushes. Now that the bush was not blooming, the house looked withered, too. The man smiled. I could swear it was Damir, Aziz's acquaintance from the service.

Aziz sighed. 'Fatima.'

I turned to him, but he wasn't looking at me, he was staring at the water, lost in his own thoughts. It was good that Aziz didn't see Damir. I didn't want to deal with jealousy. I touched his arm to get him to look at me, and asked, 'What is it?' I looked back to the fence, but Damir was gone.

Aziz looked me full in the face. 'The girls you stoned.'

'I only threw four or five pebbles at them and only one hit.' I smiled. 'But that one was a bull's-eye.'

'I should've done something.'

'I overreacted. Of course you couldn't just rush off and avenge me.'

'I'm scared her brothers will do something bad to you. I hear awful stuff about those blokes. They're killing Bosnians on the other side of the mountain. One of them was made an officer. It won't take long before they start killing around here.'

'But those girls beat me up, fat cows. And the other girls were just cheering, like it was a game.'

'I should've done something. Then they'd kill me instead. Who'd care, I'm a freak anyway.'

'Stop that! Please stop it! It's eating me alive. You're my freak and I'm your freak. And I'll beat up that bitch again if she so much as sneers at me.'

Aziz pressed his lips together tightly. 'It's not funny. Grow up Fatima.'

I stood up and slapped him. An immaculate blow. He didn't budge but gave me that damn pitiful look, as if the message was garbled and needed translation. I lifted my hand to deliver another blow, but I refrained. He looked through me. I returned his lugubrious gaze, then left. What else could have happened?

Death. Two deaths. A funeral. Imam Atif was killed, and Nisveta, the rainbow woman, just plain dived from the cliff above the waterfalls. I went there the moment I heard about it. There was a torn cardigan splayed between the rocks where the falling stream looked like churned milk. I decided it was the last damn time I'd go to that beautiful but wretched place.

Imam Atif was reciting the night *edan*, prayer call, when a crowd of civilian men came, closed him into his little office, and mined the mosque. The explosion shattered the windows of the houses around the mosque and made witnesses deaf for days. The next afternoon, we heard about the detonations going on in Banja Luka. The Serbs were holding the city and there were no fights against them whatsoever, but they still blew up a couple of cafés owned by non-Serbs. They razed sixteen ancient Ottoman mosques within a matter of days; one of them was called Ferhadija or Ferhat-Pasha's mosque and was over three hundred years old, situated close to the Kastel castle. It took three centuries of wind, rain, quakes, and two world wars to shape it, and one local to raze it. It wasn't enough to empty the place of the Muslims; they were purging Balkan history for the sake of their future generations. They wanted to erase every trace of a whole culture.

The town was strangely silent about the blowing up of the mosque and the imam's death. It was such a simple and clear evil, and all chatter ceased. The entire mosque building was levelled except for the minaret, which looked like a broken pencil.

It was a small funeral on a genuinely funereal afternoon. Ice-cold showers washed sad, but not crying men. Few came; most people had already left the town, through the woods or by bribing their way out; some of them were just too scared. I was there, but no other women were there. Women didn't go to funerals, because they wept and swayed their bodies and pointed thin fingers to the sky and prayed out loud and cursed too loudly. That was what men said they did. I cried for that scarred woman, but didn't make a fool of myself. Father was there. Aziz was there with his father. Even his brother Weasel came, but he didn't speak to Aziz.

Aziz's brother said to my father, 'It's good that she died. Her life was meaningless after her Suljo died. She wouldn't come out and be with people. There was never any smoke from her chimney.'

Father added, 'She'll be better off, wherever she is now. She had a good share of burns in this world. I hope she'll skip hell.'

I listened to them talk, but I didn't say a word.

First, all the men carried Nisveta's body on the *tabut*, covered with a dark green cloth, and then they brought Atif's remains. They always did it that way: take hold of the *tabut*, carry it a short time, then give way to somebody else, using the time while carrying the body to pray for the deceased soul. Aziz wouldn't give up his spot under

Nisveta's *tabut* to anybody else. He carried her all the way to the hole as if to make sure that, when the time came, God would ensure that someone like him would want to carry his body all the way down to the cemetery.

The prayer was short. Since there was no other imam, one of the older and learned townsmen acted as stand-in. He had a French cap slightly tipped backwards and a green cape over his black suit. His face looked like a crying statue, like one of those saint figures the Catholics say sometimes cry blood. Few answered 'Yes' to the man's closing question: 'If anybody holds a grudge against them, if they owed you money, or if there's anything else, will you forgive them?'

I thought, No. Nothing to forgive.

Father went into Nisveta's grave and put five broad planks at forty-five degrees over her body. Aziz reached him a hand and pulled him up but they didn't exchange looks. Everyone threw a shovel of soil into the hole. After all the men had done so, Aziz and Father filled in the rest of it.

The following night, Aziz and I were sitting in his garret glued to each other, watching his empty street. People avoided going out. Most of the townsmen, especially those who lived near the mosque, had nailed planks on any windows that faced the streets, because of the regular drive-by shootings. Every hair on my head cracked at the roots when Aziz's mother Behara came in. I pulled myself apart from Aziz and cringed on the other side of the sofa. Her face was moist, as if she had a fever. She pushed Aziz aside and glanced through the window. He raised his hand to caress a lock of her brown hair that hung out of her scarf. She turned swiftly, her pink nose an inch from his. She licked her thumb and stroked his eyebrows and said, 'Aziz, hurry; they'll be here any minute.' Then she sniffed him. 'You haven't changed your clothes. You can't go around like a stable boy all the time.'

I looked at her submissively but didn't move an inch. She was beautiful in the old-fashioned outfit, with a big grey skirt tied above her bulky stomach, and a tight dark blouse with falling layers of lace along the collars. Her white scarf with blue and red needlework along the sides was tied around the top of her head. I said nothing. She beckoned with her hand, and as she was closing the door behind her, she said, 'What are you two waiting for? Aziz, go and wash yourself! I've left you a white shirt in the bathroom. You can't be dirty at the dinner table.'

He nodded.

Later, the front door swung open to reveal a short, hefty man. He had black stubble and a burnt face. His eyes bulged beneath his bushy eyebrows, which looked like an extra moustache. Three boys crowded in front of the man. I smiled. They were smaller copies of their father, all four tarred with the same brush. The sight of the boys made me glad. They had nothing of their mother's soft posture. It was obvious she wore her best pink blouse and a dark blue skirt with a brown cardigan down to her knees. She smelled of burnt sugar.

Aziz's mother said, 'Welcome, welcome. Do come in.'

'*Salaam-u-alaykum*,' the man and the woman said, and the kids chanted the same a second later, only almost silently.

'*Alaykum-u-salaam*,' we said.

Behara bent down and faced the children. She pinched their cheeks and said, 'Oh, don't be afraid, come in, I have some nice sweets for you.' She'd spoken it so loud they jumped back and grabbed their parents' legs

'They're shy with people they don't know. But don't worry, next thing they'll be jumping around the house.' The woman's voice was both shrill and weak, as if she was hoarse by nature.

'Oh, we don't mind lively children. It's time this house saw a few,' Aziz's mother said, rolling her eyes at me. 'But look at us. We're standing at the doorstep, instead of going inside.'

'My name's Irfan.' The man reached out his hand.

Aziz's father shook it, saying, 'I'm Ibrahim.'

'So rude of me not to introduce myself first, I'm Behara,' Aziz's mother said.

Irfan pointed as he said the names of the others, 'This is my wife, Zumra, and the boys are Amir, Amar, and Amel.' We all laughed.

'And this is my youngest son, Aziz. We're fond of 'A' too. And…' Behara waited a little as if she was trying to remember if she'd forgotten anything, and then said, 'And this is my future daughter-in-law, Fatima.'

'Oh how nice. *Mashallah*. Congratulations.'

'Nice to meet you,' I said, and Behara only contrived a smile.

At dinner, the boys wriggled in their chairs. Their shyness was gone. Their mother smiled slightly at us and at the same time gave her sons furtive looks, to make them sit still. She was simmering while her man chatted with Ibrahim. Both men were chewing smoked mutton, noisily smacking their lips, and sipping their brandy. The woman's face twitched and she pressed her hands against each other.

'Don't worry about the children, dear,' Aziz's mother said. 'They're still little. Big children big trouble, people say.'

The woman only nodded. She gazed over the dirty plates and cutlery in front of us. Bigger plates and casseroles crowded in the middle. There was lots of pita, pastry filled with minced meat, pumpkin, spinach, and cottage cheese. There was a big, opaque bowl of plum compote, a few small bowls with whipped, salty cream mixed with chopped tomatoes and green blades of onion. Behara was exceeding their means, but it was wonderful. Living in the moment.

Afterwards, I thought the finished dinner was a sorry sight. All the smells and tastes that a moment ago raised my spirits were gone. Aziz silently chewed on his last piece of meat. I knew he hadn't eaten this well for months, and neither had I, but mostly because my appetite was worthless and my stomach was killing me.

Behara said, 'Now, it's late and you probably want to get some rest. I've made all the preparations'

The woman said, 'You're so kind Behara; I don't know how to thank you.'

'Nonsense, don't be silly. We have space. You'll be sleeping upstairs. Only there's no toilet there, so you'll have to come down here when you need it.'

'Thank you. We hope our home will be free soon, so we can pay back your hospitality.'

'Let's hope it won't come to that,' her husband said. We all winced. The light from the brass oil-lamp at the windowsill was faint and the two men were in a penumbra, so his voice seemed even darker. 'I meant that when this war ends, we could visit each other like friends. I hope we will.' He dabbed at his mouth with his napkin. 'You know, just a month ago in Prijedor, we thought we'd be able to stay put much longer, but when the Serbs moved in we found ourselves with another group of refugees. We didn't have a plan. At least we didn't end up in the Karaterm concentration camp. We were so lucky. And now we're eating with you as if it's peace.' He smiled and ruffled the eldest boy's hair. 'But soon we'll all have to move again.'

'Dear friend,' Behara said. 'I wish this war never happened, but we'd never meet if it weren't for it. My parents met during last war. It was fate.'

The woman covered her face with her palms. Rivulets welled from under her hands, more and more with every sob. Her husband bit his lower lip. The woman pressed her hands against her face. Behara stroked them and took them from the woman's face, revealing one already corrugated eye, with long black lashes glued to the skin around them. Behara kissed her hand.

I dried my eyes in a sweep, stood up, and said, 'I'll show the boys to their beds, if that's all right.'

Nobody said a word. I nudged Aziz. The boys dived under the table, went through a maze of legs, and ran out, showing us their little tongues. We inched out of the kitchen, and then dashed after the boys. Aziz took two of them under his arms and carried them out into the backyard. They giggled, while the third one made faces at us. He put the boys down and ran off to fetch a ball. 'Who's my buddy?' he cried. I felt like kissing him, he was so great that moment.

'Me, me, me!' the boys yelled, jumping around like oversized rabbits.

'Okay, if you're good, tomorrow we'll—' Aziz didn't finish because the tallest boy, Amir, kicked the ball over the neighbour's fence. Aziz stood peering into the darkness. The boys gathered around him and tugged at his sleeve. 'We're sorry.' Aziz smiled faintly.

I said, 'It's all right, kids. Come on, I'll show you your room.' We scrambled up the stairs to their room. Aziz ambled after us.

Tightening the Belt
(Winter 1992-93)

Aziz was like a rib I'd torn out of my body. It was bent like a soft penis, yet hard. I've never been able to make it straight, for fear it would break.

At the beginning of the December of the same fleeting 1992, the war was blossoming and Aziz and I didn't have sex for two months. We had other things to think about, like escape. On Christmas morning, we went to fetch some humanitarian aid from Merhamet and Karitas. There we were, short of everything. No Muslim, Croat, Gypsy, Jew, or any other nationality but Serbian could earn money in any honest way. The saving accounts, which were holes in the floors stashed with money, gazed back at us like new-hatched chickens. Little by little, we bartered furniture, cars, jewels, and animals with the Serbs who were still willing to pay, and not just come and pillage. And pillage they did, a house or two every night. Those were small groups of regular people. Not military. The real soldiers were busy killing and burning elsewhere. We didn't resist. How could we? With what weapons? Hayforks and kitchen knives?

That day, the strangest thing happened. We went to fetch some humanitarian aid from the Merhamet station. When we got there the manager told us, 'The damn UNICEF brought in humanitarian help for children, clothes and boots.' We didn't understand his anger until he showed us the labels from the boots: Proper boots keep you healthy. Step out into happiness in shoes from Belgrade. The goods were from the aggressor country Serbia. Incredible. And what was worse, the things were paid for by UNICEF. Idriz, the manager at Merhamet, said, 'We returned the gifts, of course.'

Aziz and I went home empty-handed.

*

Aziz and I sat on the Rainbow Bridge. I thought I'd never come back here after Nisveta's suicide but I did. I looked up at the cliff above the waterfall. The mountainside made the churning water look insignificant, like tears nobody ever sees but which go on running, just in case. There was something threatening and sad about waterfalls, as though it was an old women who believed she could have long hair again as once upon a time. They'd put on their scarves as if for religious reasons, but really it was to hide what time did to their hair.

On the mountain there were four-hundred-year-old Ottoman ruins. At the top there was a low remaining wall of a bastion, but a little farther down towards the waterfalls there was a prison. You couldn't go inside because it was filled with soil; the outside shape looked as if it had grown out of the rock. Aziz looked down, and feeling dizzy from the height, moved closer to me.

'Aziz, we must leave this place, or we'll die. My father won't even hear about it.'

'Has something happened?'

'I went to school the other day.'

'You didn't tell me.'

'Mum made me. She said the situation is still uncertain and we may be spared. She didn't want me to miss out on anything. And then the damn teachers talked about how it was the prime time for real subjects to be taught, like Serbian history, Serbian as the mother tongue, Serbian this and Serbian that. By the end of the day I thought even mathematics would be called Serbian. And the blokes only talked about guns and something called AK that they found on their doorsteps one morning. They said every Serb family found one on their doorsteps.'

'I heard something like that from the refugees. It was the same in their village. First, the Serbs distributed the AK47 rifles to everyone.'

'That's right, AK47.' I held his hand and scratched between fingers. 'On the way home, a few of us were crossing the bridge over Vrbanja. I don't know if these blokes followed us from school, or if it was spontaneous, but they hurled themselves at us, screaming curses. Their faces were knotted up like fists because of their hatred.'

Aziz was silent and he looked in the other direction, but I knew he was listening.

'They didn't hit anybody at first, just yelled and insulted us as if they wanted to pick a fight, but we ignored them. They gathered in a circle, talking and laughing. We hoped we could just walk on.' I picked at my cuticle. 'Then they lined up in two rows and dashed at us, making the sound of a train. It was so surreal.'

'But what happened?'

'They grabbed Denis, and before we realised what was going on, they threw him off the bridge. Just like that, like a pebble you hurl into water when you're bored.'

He wiped his eyes. 'They did nothing to you?'

'No, because I ran like mad, until I couldn't breathe.'

He put his arm around me. He kissed me on the temple, and then said, 'My parents are stubborn too. They'd rather die than leave. The refugees from my house are already whispering about going away. Maybe we could follow them.'

I looked at him in disbelief, and then smiled as if I had sloughed off a second skin.

We walked back up my street. I led him towards a shed Father built a year earlier for hay. The snow began to fall. Otherwise, it was just an average afternoon in my street: people passing by, no one laughing; some man was yelling at his horse, which was struggling to pull a cart overloaded with firewood; women were coming back from the bazaar, dragging bags full of nothing; children soiling their clothes, running to their houses, rushing back and waving with buttered slabs of hard bread; dogs barking yelping squeaking when they were chased by the kids; cats lying silently on broad fences between people's estates, like small guardian sphinxes. All as if the word 'war' had never been broken over anyone's tongue.

The street was situated between two hillocks like a riverbed. The Rainbow Bridge was on the other side of the hill. I scampered down a slope. Aziz followed after me. We leaned on the woodshed, smelling the hay inside. There was a wasp nest glued in a corner above Aziz's head, but the insects had left. Smart creatures.

Someone down in the street cried, 'Fight!' All the boys and girls within a three-hundred-meter radius were sucked into a ring around two fighters. Then, before anyone could say 'jiffy' the fight was over. The children ran off when a panting horse headed straight at them, its head almost buried into the ground like an ostrich. The man cried out shrilly, 'Jihaah, lad, jihaah! Up with the head! Jihaah!' and as he passed the youths, 'Children, get lost!'

The kids jumped down to the feeble creek that flowed alongside the road; the man scooped up a mug of water, drank it, filled another one, and poured it over the horse's forehead. It snapped open its big black eyes, shook off the water, neighed as if it was going to increase its pace, and then dropped down on its front legs. The children ran around it, ignoring the glowering looks of the owner, and imitating the man's voice, 'Come on, lad, come on!' The man lashed the animal over the groin. It sounded like breaking glass. The horse jumped up and pulled onwards. The kids vanished.

I turned to Aziz, and was startled by his look – piercing and unpleasant. I waved my hand close to his eyes. He said, 'I hate people who hit horses.' He briefly pressed his lips together, and then burst out, 'Motherfucker!' The force of his anger unmoored him; it was one of the few times I'd heard him swear. Rivulets trickled down his cheek, tears or melting snowflakes, I couldn't tell.

I poked Aziz and he chased me around the stable, every now and then swimming into the deep white cover that was growing thicker all the time. The snowflakes, as big as a child's fists, swarmed in the sky as if it was their last chance to fall. Aziz cast clumsily made snowballs that exploded into thousands of shiny feathers as they hit my back and vanished like fireflies in the air.

Making love or war in deep snow isn't a very good idea. That became clear to many famous and infamous lovers and warriors. One willingly or unwillingly dives into the freezing water beneath the cracked crust of ice, or the crust of frozen words and sentiments. Soon enough the struggling parties realise they have to withdraw to warm shelters. We barged inside, and tried to bounce against the soft hay. I wriggled in the tickling bed, which smelled of home. All the pleasure, all the indifference to the matters of the world was too overwhelming. I smiled and pulled wry faces at my tall, laughing lover as he shook snow from his ruffled hair and dried the water from his face with his sleeves. He ripped off his saggy green sweater, torn at the elbows, and he roared like a comic book hero.

He surrendered at my side, and looked at the ceiling. The snow had ceased to fall and the clouds dispersed, the sun crept through a few broken tiles and tickled our faces like the hay. As if some open sesame magical word had glided down with the brightness of a sunbeam over my body, I lifted my head and leaned on his chest, my small toes playing with his naked feet. I saw the bulk in his crotch. I looked into his daydreaming face and said, 'Come here!' Clumsily, I dragged up my thick, wool skirt, revealing the missing knickers. His reverie disappeared. Not hesitating, not even for a split of a second, he jumped up, unbuttoned his trousers, and leaned upon me, anchoring into my warm embrace and releasing the sound of pleasure of a lost explorer who finally fell upon land. I moaned and dragged him hard into myself.

Afterward, we lay content, he on me, our bodies twitching from time to time until our limbs relaxed and we turned on our sides. I watched his closed eyes and his face muscles contracting as if in pain. He said, 'We'll be fine, you'll see.'

Then as if our contentment was too much happy time for the day, the ground shook and the stable rattled. We barged out of the wafting hay dust, pulling on our clothes and stumbling. Two pillars of smoke rose from the top of the mountain above the rainbow bridge with the speed of wind and were braided into one tower, which then diffused as it reached higher into the clear sky. Aziz hugged me and turned his back towards the place of detonation, shielding me from the scene with his body. Then volleys sounded within the black smoke, with the typical ra-ta-ta-ta-ta sound. I grabbed Aziz's fingers and pulled him forward. He jerked his hand back. 'Where do you think you're going? Are you mad?'

'Fuck everything, I'm not afraid, I want to see the bridge, I want to see the river.'

He clamped his mouth shut and followed. I bet he didn't believe I could run faster than he could, but I did.

Earth, stones, and twigs from the old buildings were strewn all over the road.

The bridge was still in place, only with a hole in the middle, the size of my whole body. I fell on my knees and hands, and snailed towards it. Aziz followed. The wood creaked and gravel rolled down into the water, sounding as if the precipice was grumbling. The edges of the hole were like a surgical cut, as if the rock that had made it was heated and burnt through the planks. I peered down and saw the rock in the shallow part of the river.

Three men laughed and kicked small stones up where the Turkish prison used to be. I screeched, 'Motherfuckers!' and the sound burst from my bowels.

'What the fuck?' One of the soldiers yelled, and shot five times, tok-tok-tok-tok-tok. The bullets hit the bridge, and Aziz coiled his arm around my waist like a boa, hitched me off the ground, and jumping with me into a nearby bush. He shut my mouth with his big palm while I was still mumbling, 'Motherfuckers.'

I didn't say a word to my parents. It took me another week to stop hearing the perfect sound of the bullets hitting the bridge. As if in defiance, or to make things seem as they were before, Aziz and I kept making love in the same stable. Or maybe we kept going there because it was such an insignificant spot that we had no fear of any drunken soldiers blowing it up.

Then one morning, Aziz's old friend Amila came to my house. I'd never really met with her before, but she talked as if we were the best of friends. She opened up completely and vomited a soliloquy. It was about that Damir we met on our trip to Banja Luka, how she was in love with him, how she was supposed to go to her aunt in Zenica and meet him there, then how she felt abandoned, how Damir was going to Germany with some blonde whores of his, then something about how much she cared for Aziz and even though she didn't like me much, she wished him to be happy. I remembered the incident in the city with the man named Damir, and Aziz's anger. Why should I care? Why tell me all of this? I said nothing, and in the face of my silence, she left. Her visit felt bizarre.

Two months later, I began to have stomach aches. Mum believed I'd lifted something heavy and disrupted my bowels. Father said, 'She's probably eaten something bad.' Due to the regular power cuts, the food spoiled quickly, especially milk, of which I drank two cups a day. We were lucky we still had cattle.

'I don't think it's the food, Rasim,' Mum said, and pointed at my face. 'She hasn't changed colour.'

'What do you suggest?'

'Fix the bowels.'

Father did the most common thing for an upset stomach. The procedure was this: he pushed up my sleeves to my shoulders, and then, with his two fingers, took hold of the soft sinew at the root of my thumb and rubbed it hard. According to old women's tales, it was supposed to set the bowels right. Then he gripped my wrist and rubbed my whole arm, up to the elbow.

It didn't help the first day. Nor the second.

Mum said, 'It's been known to work.'

Father said, 'I told you it was food poisoning.'

Mum was to-ing and fro-ing in my room like a sentry. I kept a straight face when she was there, but when she was gone I grabbed the first thing on hand and bit it to get rid of the pain. Nothing worked, and the pain continued to torture me. Nights were the worst. The light disappeared early and, without power, there was nothing to do, there were no distractions like TV or radio, so I could only go to bed. The pain wasn't the kind that made me claw at the walls. It was dull and simmering like hot milk.

Three days later, I started to dry heave. I choked with every retch, doubled over, swaying my head. There was no controlling the violent contractions of my empty stomach. I wanted to drink and eat, just to have something to throw up: water, tea, whatever could pass down my tired throat.

Mum was everywhere, bringing me salt water, sweet water, sour milk, crumbled cornbread in fatty milk. She brought warm, oiled cloths to wrap around my stomach, but I wouldn't let her get close to it. My skinny arms pressed hard just below the ribs, as if to make sure nothing was in there.

'My God, girl, what's wrong with you?' Mum was flustered. 'Where's that father of yours when we need him?'

She went for the door just as it opened, and she bumped instead into Father's chest. He said, 'Right here. What do you want?'

'Thank God you're back. Fatima's ill. She's been——'

'Fatima!' He ran to me, deaf to Mum. 'Come here little rainbow.' He scooped me up, asking no questions as he lunged for the door. 'You get her clothes and a bottle of the twice-distilled brandy from the cellar.'

'What? Twice-distilled?'

'Behind the brine barrel, wrapped in oily rags. And no fucking questions.'

By the time we reached the street, we heard her bumbling out the front door with a cloth bag in her hands.

'Hurry,' he cried.

Father paid Elvis a handsome sum to take us to Banja Luka. Elvis was the only one in town who was still brave enough, or had contacts enough, to drive around.

At the city hospital, Mum was desperate, clutching the cloth bag with the bottle of brandy. I lay on a stretcher in the emergency room. Although I'd been supine on it for an hour, the stretcher was still cold. The room was chilly and disinfected and rather empty of scissors, gauze, alcohol bottles, stethoscopes, and most of the other stuff I expected to see there. It was sickly clean, yet it seemed old and dirty.

I had a perfect view of the people on the other stretchers in their many postures of pain, sprawling, sitting, or bending over. A soldier in a stained uniform, with a bald and scarred head, sat next to another man in uniform who was soaked in blood. The sight of blood distracted me from the 'Shit happens' T-shirt he was pressing against his ribs. I retched a little.

Three noisy kids jumped around a woman with a belly that reached up to her teeth. Her dress was pulled up and even though it was freezing in the room, she was fanning herself between her legs.

An old grandma with a black knit cardigan over her head and her nails between her teeth silently moaned and dangled her legs from the sides of the stretcher.

The staff went in and out with their blank faces, assisting this or that patient. With their every move, my parents squirmed in their chairs. A nurse asked the wounded soldier, 'How are you?' His friend opened his mouth to answer, but before he could say anything, a doctor plunged in, flailing with arms that reached down to his kneecaps.

He said, 'Why do you folks come 'ere? Don't you 'ave your own medics? We can't 'ave everybody coming in 'ere just because they feel like it.' He spoke as if his mouth was full, and as all typical Serbs he swallowed 'H' sound. A semi-extinguished cigarette hung miraculously from his bottom lip, wiggling with every word he spoke. The cigarette left a trail of throat-itching smoke. I winced and buried my knuckles into my stomach. I retched. The doctor looked at me, his pupils barely visible behind the clinched lids. He had swollen, cardboard eye bags. He scratched his stubble, giving me a casual 'Mm,' before turning back to the soldiers. He hissed, 'So what the 'ell's your problem?'

The unwounded soldier said, 'We were in a minefield and it fucking went wrong. They told us to drive 'ere.'

'I don't care. I can't 'ave both civilians and soldiers around.'

The pregnant woman called to the doctor, 'Please, help us. We've been here for four hours.'

The doctor turned and walked to her. The kids went silent and grouped around him. He muttered to the nurse, 'Take those two bums out of 'ere.' He pressed his stethoscope to the woman's stomach. ''ow often now?'

'Not at all. But the water's broken.'

'All right.' He beckoned to one of the nurses. 'You! Nurse!'

The nurse nodded twice but continued pushing a stretcher with the soldier.

The doctor's brows furrowed. 'Nurse!'

'Yes?' She chewed her cheeks, her eyeballs roving the room.

'Cut that shit and let 'is pal do that! Take this woman upstairs. Give 'er a drip and I'll be right with you.' He pulled on his cigarette, and with a puff of acrid smoke, said, 'And tell Jelena to be there in ten minutes. I might 'ave to do the capital C.' Turning back to the woman, he lowered his voice. 'Don't you worry, we'll give you the royal treatment.'

He next knelt beside the old woman and still he was taller than she was. 'Now you.' He took her right leg in his hands, forming it like in a press. She mumbled every time he

pulled, pushed, twisted, or turned the bone, which was covered with loose, hanging skin. Another man in white came in, a stethoscope hanging from his neck; his arched nose looked as if it were resting on the spiky bush beneath it. He stood beside the old woman. His hands, half in his pockets, made his white coat look almost straight and ironed, but it was stained in places, with torn seams and missing buttons. He leaned forward. 'What's it going to be?'
'We'll 'ave to cut. Make it an inch below the knee. Or no, wait. It's better if we take it off just above the knee, for precaution's sake.'

My stomach ache diminished with every word the doctor uttered. As 'precaution' passed his lips, I bolted upright. I couldn't remember having felt better in my whole life. I whispered, 'Mum, I feel much better. I think it's gone.'

'We can't go before he's examined you,' Mum said.

The doctor turned to us, pushing out words through his cigarette to his colleague, 'I'll check this girl, too. And, all newcomers will 'ave to wait until the next shift comes.' As he stood over me, his index finger was pointing right to my open mouth. I retched again. He grunted, 'What's wrong honey?'

'Nothing,' I said, praying to God not to retch again. I turned over from the pain, holding my knees tight to my stomach.

'She's been—' Mum began, but Father was faster: 'She's been vomiting all day.' He gave Mum a stern look.

The doctor unhinged my fingers and pulled my legs down. He pressed on the right side of my crotch. I didn't budge.

'Are you sure it doesn't 'urt 'ere?'
'Yes.'
Mum tugged my sleeve. 'Tell the doctor, my girl.'
'It doesn't.'
'Only up 'ere?'
'Yes.'
'The other side?'

I twitched. 'No.'

'Sometimes the symptoms are misleading. Nevertheless, it could be the appendix. We might want to remove it anyway.'

'Do whatever you must,' Mum said.

'We'll 'ave to do the X-ray first. She can stay overnight.'

Father reached for the bag Mum was holding and put it in front of the man. 'Thank you, doctor. A small sign of our appreciation. We trust you'll see to it that she makes it fine.'

The doctor winked, pulling a corner of his mouth aside. He blew a short breath through his nose and shook Father's hand by the fingers. 'Of course,' he grunted indifferently, while giving him a reassuring look. Then he sniffed and left the room, his hands hanging from the stethoscope.

Mum kissed me all over the face. 'You be good and do what you're told for once.' I waited until she turned away to face the doctor, and I wiped my face dry with my sleeve.

Father kissed me, too. 'We'll be here first thing in the morning.' He looked as if he was having a hard time keeping up his mask of trust in the staff. His face was carved with worry. He took Mum's hand and they left.

Next morning, I felt terrific. The ache vanished and the X-ray machine broke down when they brought me to it, so I went home before they did something worse to me. The doctor told my parents that swollen or ruptured appendices don't just stop hurting overnight.

I overheard Father talking to Mum, 'You saw they treated her nicely.'

'Rasim, those were doctors. They don't drive around and shoot.'

'I'm sure the war will be over soon. Trust me Safija. This is our home. We'll never be safe if we leave anyway.'

She started crying and kissed him on the mouth. She bit his lower lip. I almost exclaimed, 'Wow!' It was the first time I'd seen them like that. After eighteen years they were finding their way back to each other. My stomach was completely silent.

Power Cut
(Spring 1993)

In spring, I was still in my winter mood. Bosnia didn't bloom like normal. It had no smells. Strange winds wouldn't stop blowing. People called those winds 'Old Farts', suggesting loss of vigour and confused minds.

For three days, military jeeps were driving around, occasionally shooting at walls facing the streets: scarecrow tactics. Many Serbs were leaving Croatia and the Serbian authorities wanted to take over our property and hand it to their own refugees. They didn't kick us out all at once. Instead, they sent thugs to drive by and shoot, terrifying people to sell everything they owned for dimes.

Father kept preaching, 'This can't go on forever.' But he knew about the houses that were pillaged, he knew about the people killed on the outskirts of the town, he knew that half the town had already left, and still he wouldn't do anything to get us out of there.

Aziz told me that the brothers of that damn girl I'd stoned had met him in the street and threatened him, saying they'd come and burn our house down, with us inside. When I told Father, he said nothing. Neither did Mum. I was so angry I clawed my tights until the skin felt numb. I didn't know what to do, so I took ten of our finest books, our hardcover collection about World War Two and Tito's resistance movement in the 1940s, and I made a pleasant bonfire in the backyard. I stood near the heat as the flames licked towards my face, but I felt no real satisfaction. I felt cold again.

Father came running with two bucketfuls of sand and put the fire out. Mum pushed me on the ground and pulled me by the legs towards the house. I let my body become dead weight, but Father grabbed me by the wrists and they carried me into the house. I didn't make a sound. My parents locked me up for three days in my room, and nailed the windows shut. They whispered outside the door, but I couldn't hear what they were saying. I screamed myself exhausted, and fell asleep. When I woke up, I found food and water on a tray next to my head, and a warm blanket over my back.

On the third morning, I leaned on the door, banged it with my fist, and when I heard them stand outside listening, I said, 'I'm sorry. Mum, I'm so terribly sorry. You know what's best for me, for us. I trust you.'

The door opened. They both took hold of me and lifted me up and kissed my face, my hair, my hands.

The following day, the walls of my room seemed to be closing in on me. I had covered them from ceiling to floor with pictures of film stars and singers; the famous, familiar faces over the pallid shades of whitewashed walls. The walls were rugged and the faces smooth and I hated rugged, but outside, I kissed the rugged bark of a linden tree on the slope behind my house. I leaned against the trunk of the linden as against a lover. Its crown was round and dense with new leaves. All the branches were strong and turned to the sky, all but the one drooping beside my head. Its leaves were overgrown with strange small pins, like parasite mushrooms bulging out, as if the tree's own seed had fallen on them, stayed, and thrived there. As if the seed had a fear of the dark soil and had clung to the parent.

The time when I'd been beaten, and stoned the culprits, seemed to come from somebody else's life. The times I sat in school, or ate a quiet meal with my family, or watched TV, were someone else's life. My mind was empty. I didn't think of Aziz, or the blokes who said they'd kill us. It started to rain and I went back inside.

I'd never seen Father cry like he did that afternoon. Mum sat beside him like a jug of lukewarm water. She wasn't used to him crying either. Normally, when he was sad, Father knit his eyebrows and pressed his lips tight into a pale line.

There was never a tear. There was nothing we could do about him now. He was angry, swearing like never before. Then, he fell silent, only to burst out again with 'fucking this' and 'fucking that.' Nobody's name was holy.

After two days of the swearing frenzy, he showed us a letter that someone had been slipped under our door. Perhaps the messenger knew what the news was and was afraid we would blame him, or her. It was uncanny to hold a real letter and not just another Red Cross message with half the text erased, the only kind that circulated freely. The message was from Father's sister in Bihac. I knew next to nothing about his other relatives, until we got the letter. Mum's story of their illicit relationship came back to me in all its vivid details. I tried to shake it off.

Father knew from the news that there was not much contact with Western Bosnia. The place was completely isolated under a blockade. Nothing went in or out – neither food, nor regular people. But this little note came out, and was addressed to Rasim.

Dear brother,
We're alive and hope you and your family are well. Mother is weak. Both Omer and Mustafa are in the Father's Army. So are their sons. I only have daughters, and we spend most of the time in a neighbour's cellar. It's big and not as damp as ours is. My husband is ill and there's not enough medication. There's no money. We haven't had any humanitarian aid for two weeks now. The children can hardly walk. I lean on walls when I try to move, or we just sit. Jasmina is well. She's the one writing this down. My hands are shaky. Nermina, my youngest (she's five), has found a little axe and goes nowhere without it. She goes from door to door and offers to work for food. Once she chopped wood for a bun.

I've found an old picture of you with your pretty wife. In it, you're eating from a big casserole in front of you. You're dipping bread into it and laughing. I don't know what it is.

Maybe potatoes with meat. Vegetables. You look so hungry and happy.

I'm writing to you now, because I'm happy. Last night, a local doctor (a Palestinian) came over with a sack of flour. He met Nermina and she asked for work. I couldn't believe my eyes when he brought it in. I cried, 'Children, we won't be hungry now.' Can you believe it, a complete stranger? Who are we to him? I don't remember even having said 'Hi' to him. People hold tight to what little provisions they have. They look at you hatefully if they think you want something from them. Every man for himself, as they say.

I hope you're healthy and have food for the day. Please come and see us if we survive. Please do.

There was no signature. Mum and I wept silently. I didn't know any of them, but my aunt sounded like someone who could have spoiled me, had she only been closer to us. Her words gave me a feeling of something alive moving in that closed place. I wished I were fearless like that little girl.

Mum embraced Father. He cursed the war and the politicians. He cursed Fikret 'the Father' Avdic for joining the aggressors and fighting against his own people. He cursed his two brothers for joining his army. He cursed the blockade and he cursed his own heart.

I thought that now he would understand that we had to run. I said to him, 'Let's get out. People are running away, stomping on everything and everybody in their way. This place's half-empty, like someone pulled the stopper out and everyone was washed away. Anyone with relatives abroad has left.'

Instead of an answer, Father closed himself in his shed, banging on wood and metal, sawing, filing, making something; I have no idea what, an ark perhaps. I only heard the noise. If he ever came back to the house, at night, I didn't see him. Early in the mornings, his banging awakened me. Mum didn't seem to care. She'd just make sandwiches and put them outside the wooden door.

I ran to Aziz. That spring, the best picture of him was stolen from the brush of the painter who cut his ear off over a prostitute: a lean figure with too-big clothes, standing absent-mindedly next to a sweaty heifer and bathing in a deluge of sunshine. That was how I found him when I entered his small garden on the always-sunny side of his rotting stable. My puppy body disappeared into his embrace and the starched silence was gone. He shivered as he stroked my face and his fingers played anxiously with the bobby pins holding back my hair. We knew how to read in each other. I looked towards the cherry door under his roof. Aziz said, 'They're planning to leave in two weeks. My parents are going to miss them a lot. They love the boys. They say only children can cheer you up in war.'

'Are we going?'

Aziz nodded. 'I'll see what their plans are.'

I couldn't leave everything to Aziz. I spent the night planning our escape, but lost my bearings time and again. Where to start? What direction to take? What to squeeze into a backpack? How to stop this whirlwind in my head? There was no foolproof map with markings of all the mines and old-fashioned traps. I thought about the string that some ancient hero used to find his way out of a labyrinth. I wished I'd paid more attention to 'Methuselah' Mehmed, my old history teacher. Only, what good would a string be in a mined maze of woods and fields with no walls and doors to lock and unlock?

Early in the morning, I had it all figured out. We needed to get travel documents, in case we had a chance to leave the country. For that we'd have to go to the city. We couldn't get them issued in the town. Mum and Father would be likely to find out before we could get away, and the Serbs in the office would probably demand a lot money, or perhaps they would insist that Father give them the house and land so they could say they didn't steal anything later. All the others who'd left had been make to sign over everything they had. That's how they got bus tickets to get out, nice and clean. Even Mum couldn't but admire the cleanliness and efficiency. To get to the city, I needed to pass a number of checkpoints scattered along the roads.

How? When? Who?

By car. No time to waste. Ask Elvis.

Right away I ran to Aziz, dragged him out in his long Johns only, and dashed to Elvis's place. We didn't find him in his big, façade-less house but in a little room slightly better than a shed. Men seemed to like being in those narrow, dirty places. I banged on the door but nothing happened. The door shrieked and opened a little. Elvis was lying over a too small bed snoring. I barged inside and shook him by the ears.

Elvis kept his eyes closed throughout the conversation, except while trying to fix himself a cup of coffee, which he did in the strangest way ever. He poured cold water over whole grains in a large casserole and put it on an uneven plate, which was mounted on a gas bottle. The jeans he slept in were cut off at the knees and he was wearing Japanese slippers over white socks. He pulled his lips back and showed us his disgusting teeth. He finally looked at me, 'I remember you.' His teeth and fingertips were now darker, like the corners of his squinted eyes. He leered. 'You need a favour?'

I was cut short. I wanted his help but was already caught in the game of 'you-come-here-now-that-you-need-me (cunning-smile) well-I-might-need-you-some-day (cunning-smile).' I wished I had the means to make things happen by myself. I opened my mouth to speak, but Aziz was faster, 'We need a ride to the city to get passports.'

'Doesn't everybody? Doesn't everybody come to me all the time? But if you haven't noticed, there's a war going on. You don't just walk into somebody's office and ask for a passport. You need connections, bribes, you know what I mean? Money talks, brandy talks, VCRs and TV sets talk. Deutsch marks, dollars, and pounds untie all tongues. These things make even the Gordian knot a child's game. Ah, I wish Damir was around. He had great contacts in the city. He could help you just like that.' Elvis snapped his fingers.

Aziz scowled at him. 'I'll sell my horse.' I was impressed.

'A horse for a passport. That'll do, unless your customer kills you, mounts that donkey of a horse, and rides off like Lucky Luke into the sunset.'

I said, 'When can you do it?'

'When you come back with the magic word.'

Aziz said, 'I'll have the money in two days.'

Elvis leered.

The following morning, I felt drowsy for hours. I had no idea what Aziz was up to, how he'd sell the horse and get the money, and I couldn't stand the waiting. Then I heard a noise and Father's body shadowed my window. He stood on a ladder, and began covering the window with planks. Without looking at me, he said, 'Fatima, fetch me a half-kilo hammer.'

I wanted to say, fetch your own damn tools. Instead, I ambled to the shed. How was I supposed to know a half-kilo hammer? I scanned the large wooden table, on which a dozen hammers of all sizes were spread over God-only-knew what kinds of tools and materials. For a moment, I stared at the place against which Aziz had pressed my back that night when we made love.

I thought there'd be something else in there, some huge monster device Father had managed to make in a stroke of genius, which would free the world or whatever. There was nothing at all there. I lifted a couple of hammers but couldn't decide. Then it was as if some divine a beam of light from the perforated roof fell on one shiny tool, making it shimmer like Thor's mighty Mjölnir. I reached reverently for the simple shape. My head began to sway and I had a sudden threatening image of a woman falling down into a lit-up pit. A feeling of loss swept over me and I recoiled, as if my whole future were crumbling to pieces. I ground my teeth and ran back to the house, blood pounding in my head.

'Here you are,' I said, as though perfectly contented, and passed him the hammer.

'Oh, great. That's the one.'

I didn't ask how he was doing. He said, 'Damn it. I don't have enough for every window. I'll leave the one in the living room uncovered. We never sit there anyway. I must finish at least this one before it gets dark.'

Mum came in with a basket of nettles she used to cook in those days, making soup or brewing tea. She told me that nettles were good for blood, to make a woman stronger. I dutifully swallowed anything she gave me. She said to Father, 'You're turning the house into a bunker.'

'Knock it off. You know the Serbs threw a grenade into Omer's house last night. He too refused to cover the windows.'

Mum looked at me. I turned away and stiffened. I didn't want her to look me in the face, for fear she could read me and see through to my secret intentions. I ran out, avoiding her eyes.

Farther down the street, I saw Aziz. His head was bent. He passed through a crowd of football-playing kids. At first, he didn't care to look at them, then he went back, mingled with them, teased and provoked them by taking the ball. He dribbled the ball around every one of them, letting them fall around him and finally scored. Like in peacetime. For a moment, it felt as if we were already somewhere else. 'Goal!' he cried. The boys didn't seem too happy. They swore and showed him the finger.

'Aziz!' I was about sixty feet from him, hoping he'd run to me. He scoured the place quickly, as if he'd been caught with his trousers down. 'Aziz!'

He bristled and said, 'Ah, it's you.'

'Nice, you don't even recognize my voice.' I wanted to wait until he came to me. He smiled. I ran down to meet him. 'What's so funny?'

'This.' Out of his pocket, he took a fistful of money. 'And there's more where that came from.'

I kissed him.

A cheaply-sold horse and a mouthful of happy smiles later, we were coughing in the cloud of cement dust from the factory that Elvis drove by near the city. It was the largest smog-producing monster that, before the war, had kept most of the population of the area in work. Work shifts one, two, three and, for the sake of exigency, a fourth one. Rolling, breaking, burning and cutting; acid evaporating into chaos on tight schedules; lost nerves and broken hearts. Its machines had consumed more sweat and blood than all the fictional villains of old folktales gathered together.

I looked into Aziz's eyes. I couldn't stop thinking how he'd actually had to pay our way out by selling his beloved horse. That's how it goes. I coughed and it cleared my mind. Aziz retched. His throat was congested with dust. Elvis was blinking as if his lids could clean the windshield, now that the wipers were broken. Aziz said, 'Why are we taking this road?'

Elvis fidgeted. 'What are you saying? I can't hear over the engine.'

'This isn't the one we took the last time we went to the city.'

'This road's the best. Fewer checkpoints and the soldiers are drowsy from all the chemicals and dust from the factory. They can't aim well.'

My stomach turned. I cried, 'Look! Soldiers!'

'What?' Elvis turned his eyes from where I pointed back to the road. 'Shit!' He braked. The car bucked as it hit the speed bump and stopped. Someone yelled outside. A face with sweat fighting its way through the layer of dust protruded through the already-open window.

A soldier hissed, 'Fucking Muslim balija!' His squinting eyes and clammy lips were an inch from Elvis' face. 'Where do you think you're going? Get out!'

I crouched behind Aziz's seat. He pretended he was having problems unbuckling. Outside, the soldier began chewing out Elvis. Aziz winked at me and got out of the car, half-hiding behind the small Golf. I peeped out through the grimy window. Aziz winked again.

The soldier yelled, 'Show me your documents!' His spit-white tongue licked his thin lips and dark stubble.

Elvis said nonchalantly, 'I wish to remain anonymous.'

I couldn't believe my ears. He's been doing this for too long, I thought. Elvis was out of his damn mind. He was starting to feel invincible, maybe even bulletproof. He was acting out this sketch a group of comedians from the capital did in their TV series. Absolutely mad, that's what this was, Monty Python mad. I hoped the finger of God would swing by and take us to the clouds.

Aziz lunged back and fell on the ground. The soldier heard Aziz tumble and pushed Elvis against the car, yelling, 'Don't move!' and went to check behind the car. He laughed when he saw Aziz cowering, then he guffawed. 'You! Come here!' He took off his rifle and aimed. Aziz got up and stood by Elvis, and the solider hit Aziz in the head. I dived between the seats. Warm urine ran down my thighs.

When I thought he'd come to inspect the car, another hoarse voice bellowed. I could hardly distinguish the words with all the bells tolling between my temples. 'Man, I 'ad a good shit. Emptied it real good. I feel hungry. Do we 'ave...what the fuck?' I was so damn curious I peered out again. A bucolic figure with a narrow face, large arched nose and unevenly cut beard appeared from behind the dusty bushes a yard away. 'Josip, what are you doing?'

'I've taken these two funny fucks.'

'Fuck that! Elvis, is everything okay?'

'Sort of, I didn't expect this bloke. My eyes were all dusty and he sure looks like you, Zoran.'

'Sure. That's my brother.'

They hugged. Aziz and Josip looked at each other. Aziz turned slowly towards the car and blinked a couple of times, as if to clear his eyes of dust, then talked some nonsense with that Josip soldier. Elvis reached out his arm to Josip. Hands were shaken all round.

'Man, you must forgive 'im, 'e's still green. The man's fucking serving the country, the greater cause.'

'Me too,' Elvis said.

'Sure you do, don't we all. Only I'd fucking rather 'ave a swig of beer with you.'

'I don't drink anymore. I turned religious.'

'Ah, that's a good one. Listen, why don't you get lost now, do whatever you need to do, fuck a whore, whatever, and buy us a few cold ones on the way back?'

'Like a bribe?'

'Sure, a bribe. If we're gonna fucking kill each other tomorrow, we can fucking wash down the same fucking dust today. A bribe sounds like a deal.'

'Fucking right.'

Rain fell, suddenly, thickly and heavily, as if it were monsoon time over the Balkans. Aziz and Elvis climbed back in the car. The engine revved half-heartedly.

Elvis put his head outside the window and into the pouring rain, said, 'See you then.' The soldiers disappeared behind the corner of the factory wall. Elvis babbled something indistinguishable. I grabbed Aziz's face from behind and pressed my head against the seat between us. He said nothing. He panted into my hands. I didn't let him go until the car passed the bridge over River Vrbas close to the Kastel ruins and finally stopped in front of the building where they issued passports. When he turned to face me I relaxed. He wasn't bleeding, just a little dirty in the face. Outside the car, he let the rain wash his face and combed his hair with his fingers. In we went.

Five hours later, we rubbed our passports like lucky charms. I looked ugly in the picture the clerk had taken.

Elvis drove back by another route. He passed through the city, driving slowly and looking around as if we were on a sightseeing tour. The city was like a haunted mind. It was beautiful and uncanny at the same time. It was discoloured, as if someone had washed the big busy streets in the same batch as the army green clothes. The car cruised by a large plaza with dozens of pigeons flying about, some eating from the hands of a big-bellied man in a whitish raincoat and a black beret. We stopped at the red light. I put my head through the window, curious about the strange, out-of-time figure. The man stroked his moustache and rapidly stuttered two names at the top of his hoarse voice, Layla and Deen. I thought he was calling out to his friends, but then two birds landed on his hands. He cooed, repeating the two names and kissing them on the beaks.

In a rush of dirty faces, untied sneakers, and flapping windbreakers, a bunch of kids came running towards him screaming, 'Alija, Alija!' The pigeons flew away. The man smiled, picked up his large green bag and pulled handfuls of sweets out of it. He didn't budge when he saw another train of puffing children hurtling towards him. He threw all the sweets into their midst. They fell on their knees and picked the sweets up like little hens.

I whispered to Aziz, 'He has a Muslim name.'

Aziz said, 'I heard about him. He's a local, good-souled freak. He'd suffered shell shock back in World War Two and now walks around the city in that coat of his like some cold-war agent with amnesia. I guess to the Serbs he's just a loony Muslim, pretty harmless.'

I didn't say anything. The whole sight of kids and sweets, and the pigeons, calmed me. The brave and mad sweets man made me feel safe.

In the evening, Aziz said to his parents, 'We're leaving in a day or so.' His mother fell down on the floor. 'My God, what will we do?' She sobbed violently. His father cringed in a corner. His pale cheeks glimpsed between his long fingers. The house was cold, clean and odourless. No longer a home.

Aziz said, 'Weasel isn't leaving. He'll take care of you until I've settled down somewhere else. I'll send for you, I promise. I wish you'd follow us.'

His mother cried, 'Go where Aziz? Leave our threshold. You're mad.' She gave me the fiercest look. 'What will her parents think of us if you steal her away?'

'I go willingly.'

She shook her head. 'She's stealing you from us. She bewitched you.'

I slumped hard against the wall and lowered my eyes. Aziz told her he loved me and something else but I couldn't hear because my heart pounded too loud in my head. Behara went on crying. I looked at her. Aziz hugged her, pressing his face against her breasts, wiping her tears. She said, 'Did you do this with her parents? Did you tell them? Did you Aziz?'

'We're going to,' Aziz lied. He held her for a long time. Then he went over to his father, took his bony face and kissed it a dozen times. The old man smiled, wiping his cheeks dry with one hand. The other hand was on his hip, as if paralyzed. I expected something like, 'Be a man, my son, and always take care of your family.' Instead, Ibrahim squinted and put his head in Aziz's lap. Aziz kissed his bald top.

Behara's look was like something from an old book; all daggers, but as she stared at me without blinking, the rest of her wrinkled face softened and tear after tear ran down the furrows. I wiped my nose, which I noticed was running, and went outside.

I was ambling back home when I heard gravel rustling behind me, then a soft voice, 'Fatima wait.' Before I could say anything, she pressed her cheek to mine, then held my face in her palms to dry her tears from my cheeks. She took me by the hand and without a word led me up the unlit street, by the ruins of the mosque, up the main street, almost all the way up to my house. The night was steamy and smelled of mint tea and Behara's salty sweat. The air was rife with high-pitched insect monotones, and the sounds of the churning river. Behara said, 'I thought you'd hurt him. You are his first and the first ones always hurt bad. I...' She scratched her left temple. 'No, this isn't about me. I think I was jealous, still am. I see that you love him even though he's...I don't even know what to call it. I'm sorry Fatima, I'm so sorry.' She slouched on the ground, and I hunched beside her, stroking the lifeless locks of hair that stuck out from her loose scarf. She went on, 'I had Aziz at home. He was born with beautiful long lashes, like a girl and, ah, you've seen it. I thought it would disappear with time. Children heal fast. I barely dared to wash him, I did it with my eyes closed, but the bigger he was, and he grew real fast, the bigger that thing was.'

I wanted to pelt back to Aziz and hug him. Every muscle in my legs hurt.

Behara went on, 'I had him circumcised in another town. I never let him have a girl before you. You stuck to him, I really thought you put a spell on him, a *sihr*, I really did; he wouldn't even look at me any longer, hug me like before. You see, he liked that Amila for a while.'

I winced. 'He liked Amila?'

'But never like you. You make him so happy. We're old and it's our time to die anyway. Please take care of him, please, like I would.'

I stared at her. My head wasn't moving but I nodded with my eyes. She smiled and pressed an old-fashioned pouch into my hands. 'I hope the money will last for a while. We won't need more than humanitarian aid. Who cares? I just hope you'll get out alive and have a family, maybe even come back when all this is over.'

I gaped at her, and then said, 'Thank you so much. That's all we have.' I lied. I'd stolen a box Mum had stashed behind a brick in the fireplace we weren't using, with lots of cash and three rings in it. Yes, and the horse-money, of course.

Behara kissed my knuckles and my finger tIps, touching my nails that were bitten to the quick. She put my hair behind my ears, and when our dog barked, she turned around and went back home.

The day we planned to go, I spent an hour with Aziz. I decided not to tell him about the money. I knew he wanted to appear a good provider and I didn't have the heart to rob him of the feeling that he'd done well for us. We tried to make sure we had it all figured out, as if that was possible, and then I went home to spend time with Mum and Father.

My head swayed when I saw my mother lying on the bed, her pasty face soaked in ever-running sweat, occasionally shuddering. Mum's bulging eyes gave me the worst shivers. I wanted to cry, 'Why did you have to fall ill now? You're ruining my damn life. What about my plans, my future? There's no time for sickness now.'

My gaze searched for something beyond the whitewashed walls and colourful tapestries; beyond covered windows; beyond houses doors backyards schoolyards; beyond fields and distant imaginary skyscrapers; beyond rivers and seas; beyond war and peace; beyond people and their petty dreams.

The feeling of utter reckless insensitivity and ungratefulness overwhelmed me. I was jerked down to earth with a choking sense of clammy guilt. My breast contracted and loosened as if being revved to life. I was all right and that was good enough for me. I went to my room and packed my stuff. Not much, though, a simple valise. Travelling light was the key. For once, I was ready to take a leap even if I was practically pushed into it.

I ambled on my toes through the hall, towards the front door, and hesitated for a moment beside Mum's door. I didn't put my ear against it for fear that I'd hear her heart beating, weak coughs, or long sighs. I kissed the doorknob, ran out of the house and towards the anxious shadow on the other side of the brook. An owl flew above us as we hugged. I once heard that when two shadows overlap they become brighter, almost scarily pale. We didn't. We appeared in the fresh midnight light of the twin crescent moons – one sickle for each of us – and disappeared into the mountain woods. The woods and the night don't discriminate between people.

Thinner than a Hair
(Spring – Summer 1993)

Aziz and I ran away from our homes in spring 1993, with the refugees from his house. In the dark, especially dark diffused by feeble moonlight, every turf and every tree looked new and uncanny. Even Aziz's broad back, his thick bones, his beardy face, and bushy eyebrows were strange. There were no human signs for confused minds. We trusted that someone in the group we joined would know the way to the free zone. One man, Mirsad, who used to be a woodsman, had some sense of direction.

That night fortune was on our side. It was a lukewarm night. No wolves were howling, or any heavy boots rustling. No guns were tinkling or rattling. No din deafened our ears. There were merely hearts throbbing, hands shaking, teeth grinding, sweat dropping, eyes bulging, and hairs rising. Aziz took an apple from his pocket, rubbed it against his jacket, and after making sure I didn't want it, munched away. He always ate quickly. Normally, I loved the crackling sound of his forceful bites into the hard, watery flesh, but this time I said, 'Stop making that noise!'

No matter what was going on in the column and in the surroundings, Aziz's eyes were always on me, like a lighthouse. He wouldn't let anything happen to me, whatever the cost. The three refugee boys, Amir, Amar, and Amel wouldn't let go of Aziz. Their father Irfan had to pull them off, but every now and then they'd sense a moment of weakness in their parents' grips, dash to Aziz and jump on him, kissing his face, hair, and arms. After another four hours, they had to be carried. Aziz took the oldest boy on his shoulders and the boy fell asleep. I carried my neighbour's baby daughter. The woman dragged along two constantly quarrelling boys. She looked as if she had a small sack of potatoes under her jacket. For the adults, there was no point in resting. We'd have enough time for rest once we arrived safely at Travnik, or wherever the night spat us out.

We avoided open spaces. When we left the town, we climbed the side of the hill that goes from the waterfalls, past Aziz's house and on the opposite side to the leather factory. It took us at least three hours to go downhill, trying not to slide over the crumbling earth between trees and through watery gullies. There was no safe way to plunge down. Instead, I had to brake all the time. One of the men said there were disguised precipices along the way. It was true. In one place, I thought the slope was ending, giving over to an enormous meadow, but I couldn't see the fifty foot wide and at least a hundred foot deep cut in the earth with a small creek that murmured deceptively deep at the bottom.

Up and down, woods and meadows, ploughed fields and distant lights, over and over again. The journey didn't attach me to the Bosnian soil, as homesick people say. The country was a profoundly strange place, a place that seemed to want to get rid of us. Like a mythical land that is alive and can react to trespassers. When people speak of motherlands, they often mean their turf, their house, and the small place in which they spent their whole lives, often without having seen any other part of the country. It seems bizarre for people from huge countries such as Russia, or China, to speak about the love of a country.

A distant explosion vibrated and I felt a trickle of lukewarm fluid against my thighs. I kept walking. My trousers would dry in no time and in the dark nobody would see anything anyway. All cats are grey in the dark.

The baby burped like an adult. She felt warm against me, inside my big green jacket with its four large pockets. It was Father's, the same one under which he'd carried me those chilly evenings when he and Mum ran over to the neighbour for coffee. I managed to synchronize my breathing with the baby's short sucks and fast exhales, only I inhaled when the tiny thing breathed out. I took in all the mellow air from the toothless mouth of that silent chick and exhaled it over my right shoulder, passing it over to the angel that jots down good deeds. The smell of her sweat was comforting. The angels on my shoulders stopped writing to smell the baby.

Rabija was the oldest person in the company. Her face was like an old map: plain, torn, blurred and ghostly. She was the only one who dared speak, 'Have you ever heard of the Sirat bridge? It's the passage that leads to paradise, thinner than a hair and sharper than a razor. A body heavy with bad deeds and debts will go over it with feet dragging. Then there will be people as light as rose petals. They will pass over it easily. Mothers and fathers who've lost their children will see them as wee birds who will pray to God until He leads their beloved parents through the heavenly gates. And He'll do it, for so He promised.'

'Rabija, this is Sirat, this road of ours, so please don't tell me there's another one,' her daughter-in-law said, dragging one of her sons by the ear. The boy was reeling in her firm grip, while his brother teased him by flicking him in the head. Yet they both kept their mouths shut.

Rabija said, 'If we walk this one properly, the other one won't be a problem.'

The woman unhooked the boy, and whispered, 'We'll cross that bridge when we come to it.' The boy clenched his teeth and, without a sound, took hold of her hanging hand. In spite of her expression, the woman seemed a little comforted by Rabija's confident words, which came slowly but irrefutably, even to half-deaf ears.

Rabija's son occasionally called the rest of us to wait for them because she walked as slowly as she talked. Every time she halted, she took time to caress her son. Once she said, 'You're like a little boy. It's in the blood.' We all stopped and turned towards her. 'Your father was just like that. He'd bring me fruit he stole from Fikret's orchard. I liked to see myself as a serious woman, even when I was sixteen. I'd chide him every time, but he was poor and he thought

Fikret's apricots were the only ones worthy of me. I think he enjoyed stealing sweetness.' Then she chanted an old *kasida* about the world in bloom and heavenly smells. Her daredevil voice carelessly broke the silence of the night. Her son scratched his head nervously. Rabija said, 'Don't you worry, lad. You'll be hearing my songs for a while and when you're sick to death of them, then I'll die.'

'Mum!'

She went on, 'Your father was a talker, which you're not. You're a good listener, like I was back then. He had such a soft voice. Sweet, too. I still miss him a lot. My other two husbands were quite reticent most of the time, as you know.'

I watched her watching all of us, longing for her to take me to bed and cuddle me. Aziz glanced at her like a thief, as if I'd be angry if he looked at another woman, an eighty-year-old one, but a woman all the same.

Our second night, I imagined Father roaming the town, crying in front of people still left, yelling at them, questioning everyone who might know anything about his missing daughter. And there was Mum all broken, entering Aziz's yard, finding two powerless people on the doorstep, the ground in front of their feet still wet because Aziz's mother had splashed a bucket of water for good luck, so that our future life would flow nicely, smoothly, and without trouble, just as water does.

On the other hand, it struck me that the scene might be different, the opposite perhaps, because I believed I'd somehow feel it if they were missing me and that every tear they shed would double in size in my own eyes. And I was not crying. Not a tear the whole damn night.

Next to me walked a nun, maybe my age. She had a five-year-old boy with her and a bag up to her barely visible breasts. Her veiled white face sparkled in the dark.

Rabija's sister, Devleta, couldn't take her eyes off the nun. Devleta was at least ten years younger than Rabija, but far more senile. She looked like a Bosnian version of the Matryoshka doll. She said, 'My child, you look like a drop of water, and you have a child.'

The nun nailed her eyes to the black soil of the forest clearing we were treading. Her white face in the black, cotton head-cover seemed to attract the light. Rabija tugged her son by the jacket and whispered something in his ear. He shook his head, rubbed his face with his palms, and walked over to the nun. 'Don't take it wrongly, please. She's an old grandma and doesn't know what she's saying.' The girl nodded and he, drawing his aunt closer, whispered, 'She's a nun, Aunty, a nun.' The woman was just as confused. With a sour face, she turned around a few times to check the girl.

I said, 'Oh, I'm so thirsty I could drink a whole lake.'

The nun took out a little bottle of water and handed it to me. Both my arms had a firm grip on the baby. We stopped for a moment so the nun could quench my thirst. Trying not to tremble and spill a drop, she slowly poured the lukewarm water into my mouth. The others passed us by. Aziz stopped to ask if everything was all right, and when he was reassured, he went on talking with the father of the baby I was carrying.

I said to the nun, 'Thanks a lot.'

'You're welcome.'

'I'm going abroad, and you?'

'Me too. To Italy, for studies.'

'No kidding? That's nice. Not me. I mean, I like reading, at least I used to, but life's a business. I'm not some princess who can feel a pea under ten mattresses. I'm going to get a life worth living with modern people in Europe, where people don't fight, but have fun instead.'

'Where?'

'Germany, or Austria, you know, any place is better than this, where everybody hates you. I'll go somewhere where you only walk in the woods for sport.'

'I wanted to stay.'

'You didn't.'

'I grew up near the Catholic Church and couldn't imagine I'd ever leave it behind like that, unprotected like a baby.'

'It's just a building. At least the Serbs didn't blow it up. You did a good thing, following the flow.'

'Doesn't mean it was the right thing to do.'

I stopped and shook my right leg to get rid of a cramp. 'Trust me, it was the best.'

We walked on. She said after a while, 'It doesn't feel like it. I could've studied Latin in Banja Luka, all the same.'

'You're running to save your skin. School is just an excuse. But, now that I think of it, how come you're here with us, walking through these wretched woods? I'm sure your people could've arranged for you to skip all this, make it smoother, you know?'

'It's a matter of heart. I wanted to make it physically difficult to leave Bosnia, as difficult as it felt inside, like a private pilgrimage away from the Holy Land. Otherwise I don't think I could do it.'

'You sure have thought it through. You're a little like Aziz. The other day, he kissed every corner of his house, every door, even the stable door; he said farewell to every animal they had: the horse, or no, not the horse, he sold it, but all the other creatures. Even the damn chickens, excuse my language.'

The nun glanced at Aziz. 'He's nice.' He looked as if he was riding a donkey and walking at the same time. The youngest boy was hanging from his shoulders.

I teased her. 'Hey! You're a nun. You shouldn't be looking at handsome boys.'

The nun wedged her gaze onto the ground and muttered something that sounded like Our Father.

I felt contrite. 'I was just kidding. Please don't be embarrassed!'

The nun sank into other thoughts and I lifted my head, feeling rather insulted that the girl was ignoring my friendliness. Then I saw a town below me. It was shining in the semi-darkness of the dawn, cosy like a romantic evening by a small fire on a riverbank. I remembered the description of this valley from Ivo Andric's book, *The Chronicles of Travnik*, which we'd read in school, and this place was nothing like it.

I looked over the hill clearings and Vlasic Mountain. The scattered roofs of small houses were lying around the cloud-white buildings in the middle. The whole place was like an enormous body lying akimbo, tired and snoring, at times shuddering and squirming in its sleep as the irregular shelling struck it here and there.

The nun said, 'How did you get that scar?'

I hardly moved my lips when I said, 'It's not a scar. It's a sign.'

'Of what?'

'I haven't figured it out yet. Not of the Devil, I hope.'

She scratched her nostrils a couple of times. 'A nice way to enter a new world, don't you think, even if it's in our own motherland. A new world in an old one. I'm ashamed to say that this'll be my first time in Travnik.'

'This'll be my first time, too. There has to be a first time for everything.'

She wiped her eyes and nose. 'There's an old Catholic school there. I'll go and see a man my tutor recommended, but I don't think I'll be staying there for long.'

'Why should you?'

'Maybe I'll fall in love with it. I've heard nice things about it.' Then, as if a lightning bolt hit her toes, the nun stopped and stammered, 'Look, Fatima, a rainbow!'

I looked over the unfamiliar countryside. I could only see some light play from the rising sun. I said, 'You like it?'

She seemed inspired when she answered, 'It came so suddenly and it will vanish as quickly as dreams when you wake up. It's inviting us to a better future.'

I sighed. 'Whatever, but then, I might just as well walk under it.'

She said nothing. Her gaze was reverently glued to the shimmering sky and her chin dropped down, her thoughts perhaps drifting down to the city under the rainbow, pregnant with the oblivion of another no-less-violent time. The slopes around it were curved like a bud, opening at the first touch of light. I tittered and the baby shuddered. I strode down, trying to stay focused on my goal and untouched by the nun's sentimentality. The others hurried after me. The baby was still sleeping. A fatigued voice sounded from an adjacent minaret, '*Allahu akbar, Allahu akbar.*'

Everyone stopped to listen. When even the nun stopped and closed her eyes, I felt I'd be rude not to stop and listen too. The voice was strong and soft, like ripples in sand. Travnik had several mosques, so different muezzins standing on each minaret never began prayer calls at the exact same time. After the first call, there was always a short delay before another. Then there would be one more, then another, then a fifth and sixth to pursue the call, like call upon call, carrying each other, connecting the peaks, rippling over the earth from its centre to the horizon. Every prayer call is personal, different in its flow.

When I snapped open my eyes, it was day already, as if I'd been sleepwalking down the mountain. I was still holding the baby and standing in a myriad of exhausted faces: shabby, smelly, loud, confused men and women, uncontrollable children playing all kinds of pranks. I couldn't see anywhere beyond the bunch pushing us around and walking in all directions, like insects looking for juice.

I gave the baby back to her wide-eyed mother, but not until I gave her one last, long kiss on the temple. Aziz grabbed my hand, shattering my first impressions of the part of Bosnia I'd probably never have seen if I hadn't been forced to flee my home. He led me straight through the crowd, ignoring other people and the screeching vehicles. He blew air through his wide nostrils, and he didn't dry the condensed water hanging from his nose. He sniffed and strode on.

I pulled my hand back. 'Aziz! Hey, stop there! Where are you going?'

He stopped and turned around. He was standing five inches away from a low iron fence with a small decaying house behind it. His eyebrows twitched, giving a hint of fear. He said, 'I thought the road forked. And this house looked so familiar.'

'So you headed for it. Going away from me already?'

He let go of the bags and slumped down onto the grass. 'Damn it, I'm already behaving like my old man.'

'You're just tired.'

'Come here.'

I laughed and stood on the spot, contorting my body in a display of exhaustion. 'I'm so tired myself I can't make it there.' Then I crashed down and rubbed my lids in one fast movement with my sleeves, but before I could wipe off the sweat itching my upper lip, I dropped my hands beside me. My face and my body betrayed me in its fatigue.

A hoarse male voice came from the incessantly moving crowd behind us. 'Look at these two! They think this is some kind of holiday. Like fucking tourists.'

I said, 'We should get going.' I felt my blood streaming up and warming my ears again. I heard a crescendo of an out-of-time orchestra of refugees concocted with the local population, foreign aid-workers, cattle and poultry. We stood up and looked down the street. Aziz stretched his arms and lifted the bags.

After we'd walked a good mile, he said, 'You know what's funny? As we walk, the street seems straight but farther away it's like a snake. You know, as if you've seen drunken drivers stopped by the police.'

'That's right.' I laughed.

'They have to walk down a straight line, a curb or something, to prove they're not drunk.'

'Yeah and now it's like we're trying to walk straight but the snaky road is winding in my head, too.'

'Still, we're managing just fine.'

We stopped in front of a post office building. It was distinct from, but glued to, a couple of other houses. The façade was crumbling and the paint on the woodwork flaking. We threw our bags down close to a group of local women and men standing there, watching the river of refugees flooding the banks of its bed. A short, bulky man with a bushy moustache leaned against the post office door and sniffed at the man next to him, saying, 'Another wave of peasants.'

I remembered my first visit to Banja Luka and the way city girls called us peasants too. I took one step towards the man, but Aziz pulled me back. I muttered, 'Let me slap him.'

Aziz whispered, 'No.' He was right. We weren't at home. Travnik was in the same small country but a new territory.

There was another man, dressed like a door-to-door salesman with a bagful of unsold junk and anecdotes that nobody wanted to hear. He said, 'They are such a nuisance; you can't go to the bakers or to the market any longer without seeing those miserable faces, or being asked annoying questions. Where's this and where's that? What the fuck do we look like, a travel agency?'

Aziz and I held hands, and listened. My palms and soles itched. I wanted to leave but more than that I wanted to hear these 'welcome speeches'. The men didn't seem bothered by our presence. I expected at least someone to see us and ask something, where we were from, where we wanted to go, anything. We helped the refugees who came to our town.

A sad, dry female voice sounded from the window above the entrance. 'You're right. We can't possibly feed all those refugees. What will happen to us?'

Her husband turned up behind her. 'What's wrong with you? Those are our own people. We're responsible for each of them. Some of them are defending this city up there on Vlasic.' He pushed her away from the windowsill, pointed towards the mountain and made a circle with his right hand. She pointed to the boisterous bazaar of refugees. 'Come on. Everybody comes here. What's this place, some kind of paradise? We're hungry, too.'

The post office seemed to be a Bosnian version of Speaker's Corner in Hyde Park. I stroked my lips. The word 'hungry' made my stomach growl and I heard Aziz's belly roaring too.

Her husband said, 'I decided to take on one family. I talked to some people.'

'You did what? You fool.' She slapped him on the head, and he slapped her back. They disappeared from the window, but I heard more yelling and hitting.

Aziz guffawed. I wanted to kiss his big white molars that always showed when he laughed so much. The moustachioed man turned towards us. He had no front teeth. He put two cigarettes in his mouth but didn't light them. He said, 'My wife and I wanted to help someone, like these two here.' He pointed at us with both his hands. 'But we're in a kind of crisis right now and as my wife always says…'

The salesman said boisterously, 'Those damn politicians. Look what they've done to us.'

The two-cigarettes man said, 'Don't tell me you put your ballot in the wrong box?'

'I sure as hell didn't, but then people are like cattle; they just don't get this democracy thing. They think it means you have the right to do anything you want. Nothing's changed, except nowadays we choose our torturers.'

I rubbed my eyes. I could hardly see anything and I could no longer listen to this damn debate. I kept seeing white sheets and soft beds. Aziz nudged me and smiled. I jerked my head as a sign we should move on. We hobbled down the street. The voices faded away.

*

None of the people from our group could navigate in the city, and after hearing that welcome conversation of the locals, I wasn't terribly enthusiastic about the new place. I couldn't see Irfan and Zumra anywhere. I thought I'd see the boys because they weren't the kind to disappear without making at least a little noise, but they were gone, too. There were a couple of people, along with the nun, heading down the street quietly. Sober locals watched the nun with drunken eyes. I elbowed Aziz. 'Let's see where they are going.'

We caught up with them. The nun smiled at me and stroked my arm. She was sweet and child-like yet her face gave the sense of experience. I came close to her and kissed her on the cheek. She smiled again.

When we took time to notice, Travnik was beautiful. The houses and buildings closer to the centre had less shell damage, but the ones close to the mountain slope were like sieves. Seeing people on balconies and in windows was bizarre. They looked unaffected, as if the crumbling walls were something natural.

The streets were narrower downtown, and the houses were glued to each other, even though they were completely different in shape. The town gave the sense of being built in irregular waves; the waviness of streets was slightly in the wrong direction to the houses, and the sky looked like a hollow ceiling. We walked by a spot where a strong stream called Lashva springs out of the mountain. Someone, a long time ago, built a series of low walls that directed the water and created small dams. The café to the left had wooden shutters over the windows.

We drank freezing water. A little farther up, a couple of women had taken off their blouses and were washing themselves. One of them had a torn bra close to the nipple. She saw me watching her and scowled.

The nun said, 'I have to move this way towards the Catholic school. It was nice meeting you.'

'Skip goodbyes, we'll probably bump into each other again. Chances are small we'll all be leaving soon.' I kissed her again and she went away. I watched her until she was out of sight. Aziz and I went to a high school where a refugee shelter was set up. It was a two-storey brick building with at least a dozen wide rectangular windows in a neat row that faced the street. Each window was divided by thick white lines into eight smaller frames. We went straight into the gymnasium to crowd in with other refugees. To make it worse, there were a bunch of kids running around and occasionally stepping on people. The room smelled of stale foot-sweat, and the way wet clothes smell when the air is moist and they never dry.

Early the next morning, a group of women, some with crosses and some with crescent badges on their sleeves, came to give us some food and water. They had soup, bread, and some canned meat. They gave us blankets and pillows and two paper-thin mattresses. Aziz and I were starving, but as soon as I brought a piece of food to my mouth, I retched. I shoved my share into my bag and Aziz did the same. He hugged me and we fell asleep.

I woke up in the middle of the night and inched out to check the rest of the school. It was dark but the strong twin moons lighted it enough so that I could navigate. The corridors were long with lockers here and there. Stench from a toilet with broken doors pushed me into an open classroom on the opposite side. The furniture was all misplaced. The teacher's desk was in the middle with two rows of small desks in a circle around it, and more were scattered around the rest of the room. There was a heap of chairs in a corner, a couple of cabinets with broken glass doors, and the remains of a human skeleton model. Its plastic, unbroken heart was on the floor.

I peered through the grimy windows. The moons looked as if they were almost touching each other. I spotted a tiny figure scampering towards the entrance. I dashed downstairs and a beam of light showed the latecomer, the nun. She sagged down when she saw me.

'The Catholic school was closed.'

'Well, step into my humble abode,' I said and bowed.

I led the nun to see her new bedroom. Her name, Dunja, meant quince, and I loved that. She looked over the gymnasium and sighed. In the dark, people were like mounds of mud after a flood. There were clothes hanging from the two handball goals. Somebody had torn off the net and glued cardboard pieces on it to make a tent. The nun smiled, tears dropping on her lips. She turned to embrace me. My legs gave up on me and I lay down right where we were standing under the doorframe. She lay beside me and buried her hands into my sweater. I stroked her face and dried off the tears. I kissed her knuckles. She whispered something about daily bread and trespasses.

When I woke up, she was gone.

Aziz and I stayed in the school for another month or so, but I did not count the days. There was food and water and a lot of cuddling, heavy snoring, farting and burping, lots of outbursts of anger and laughing. I didn't know what provoked the laughter that came from the other side of the hall, but it sounded great to my ears.

We spent most of our time muddling along in the city. At least once a day we'd drink water from the Lashva spring and afterward wash ourselves. Still we couldn't take a proper shower for another month. To make matters worse, someone snatched our bags so that we had no clothes to wear while washing the dirty garments.

A week later, two women came, dressed like secretaries in smooth cotton suits with thin white stripes, but their hair looked like bird nests, every hair sticking up or down in a different direction, bushy in places, flat and greasy in others. Their breaths smelled of tobacco and peppermint.

When it was my turn to talk to the women, a group of soldiers came and pulled Aziz aside. Out of the corner of my eye, I watched as they talked to him and some other men, but I was half-listening to those two women, who were from some organization I couldn't remember the name of. I tried to figure out what those soldiers were telling Aziz because he smiled and nodded vigorously. The women's voices droned in my head, but the only thing I could think of was Aziz's deformity. I knew those fuckers were trying to put a rifle in his hands and my greatest worry was what our own soldiers would do to him when they discovered he had more than a penis under that zipper.

'So what do you think,' one of the women asked.

'Think what?'

'Don't make fools of us, we're here with good intentions and you two look like you're starting a family. This place would be a nice solution for your problem.'

'Problem?'

The other woman asked, 'Are you all right?' Then she realised I was watching Aziz and the soldiers, and said, 'Oh, don't worry. If he gets into the army, you'll have enough provisions. The army's quite generous.'

'And Zenica isn't that far,' the first woman said. 'He'll be home quite often.'

'Zenica,' I said, having no idea what they were talking about. 'Sounds okay to me.'

Before we knew it, we were settling into the so-called Norwegian refugee facility in Zenica, a city some forty miles from Travnik with the Vlasic Mountain and other high peaks in between. There, we met the girl we'd share our one room with.

Settling and Unsettling
(Autumn 1993)

'Always look at the bright side of life,' I whistled the Python tune and stared at the naked walls of our half of the room in that Norwegian refugee camp in Zenica. The camp was nothing like home, but then who'd think it would be. It was okay, though; a couple of nice barracks, impervious to wind and rain, a genuine shelter. We were rationing our money in case we needed to bribe someone to smuggle us abroad. We didn't really know how things worked. Then we heard that the Serbs in our hometown had put everyone who was willing to give up their legal rights to their property on busses for Scandinavia. I nearly bit off my thumb. We had planned badly. I thought, maybe Father finally came to his senses and signed over the house and all our land for two tickets to Sweden. I felt so stupid that I had left. Stupid and hungry.

Those first days, before Aziz went off to shoot people, we walked around, checking the city. Most buildings were higher and had darker façades than those in Travnik. The locals said it was because of the steel works. Those grey monsters were practically right inside the city.

On September 11th, the day before Aziz was going back to Travnik and up to the mountains at Vlasic, the city was full of dust. The street asphalt crumbled under all the heavy artillery that passed through, and the air was clogged. Aziz said, 'It reminds me of the gravel road that leads to my house.'

My stomach acted up as we passed a store. We'd had a good breakfast that morning so we had no intention of going inside. Then, lorries rumbled down the street raising clouds of dust. We went inside the store to escape. The store was half empty, or even less than that. On the smudged glass counter, there were three loaves of dark bread and some twenty jars and tins spread all over the wooden shelves. Hearing our coughing, a skinny old woman with a simple white scarf on her head rose from behind the counter and said, 'I thought when the steelworks were shut down the air would get better.'

I wiped my lips with my sleeve and looked at her.

'Can I help you?'

I glanced at Aziz; he was digging in his pockets, deeper and deeper, but that gold mine was pathetic. He pulled out one bill and a few coins. 'What can we get for this?'

'Four loaves of bread.'

I said, 'How about some jam, whatever you have, plum or apple.'

'There's some rosehip jam left. I can get you a small jar and a quarter of a loaf for that money, if you'd like.'

We said together, 'We'll take it.'

In the evening, we occupied our joint kitchen and pulled the curtain all the way to avoid our roommate's leers. I wiped the small table with my T-shirt and Aziz cut the bread. I spread the jam with my forefinger and let him clean it with his lips. Our eyes met and I said, 'I could eat this rosehip jam and bread until I die.'

'Me too.'

So we had a good plain dinner before Aziz's first departure, the next morning. He was to be stationed somewhere in the forests of Vlasic. What else could he do? He figured it would at least provide food for the table, and he would have the perks of a regular job. He never asked what I thought about his becoming a soldier, a defender of the country. My first impression was that I thought he was handsome in the uniform with the blue-white badge on his shoulder; and on his cap, the new Bosnian symbol, a large silvery lily, a French lily. The following day, a soldier called Ziki came to the camp to fetch Aziz. He drove an antiquated VW Golf. After Aziz gave me a well-deserved goodbye kiss, I said, 'You look ugly in that uniform. I bet you the damn Chetniks will fall dead, that's how ugly it is.

You won't have to shoot.' What I really wanted to say was, 'Don't be a hero. You have nothing to prove.'

All the while he was gone, I stayed alone in the camp; confined to the room we shared with Alma, a skinny girl from Brcko, a place in northern Bosnia. Unlike the other people from her hometown, she'd ended up in Zenica in eastern Bosnia, and not in one of the transitional refugee facilities along the Croatian bank of the river Sava. Alma was a spunky little brunette, peppered with freckles. Even her teeth were mottled, from chain-smoking and coffee. She was terribly restless, and always mulling over the same desires for money, a singing career, big houses. Not much different from other people's dreams, including my own. At least I was realistic about my singing talents. Alma would sing to me from time to time, like some old-timer crooner. She started off out of the blue, 'Sta ce mi zivot bez tebe dragi' ('What's life without you, darling?'). Then she hit the little table in our joint kitchen like some stereotypical drunkard. She was touched by the tune and wanted to break a glass against the floor, and then lift her arms in slow motion, carried by the music and lyrics. Only we didn't have glasses to spare for these kinds of moods, so Alma only pretended to do it.

She was good to us at first. She was a hooker.

Aziz came home on his first leave of absence three weeks after he'd left. 'I can stay for two nights.' I made a face and pushed him on the narrow bed. 'Three times seven equals twenty-one. You have two nights to make those up to me.'

He laughed and said, 'I'm thirsty. Can I have a glass of water please?'

'You can drink tomorrow. You haven't earned it yet.'

I jumped on him and for one whole night didn't hear Alma's hooting.

In the morning, I went to fetch Aziz a glass of water. Alma winked at me. 'Someone got lucky last night.'

I ignored her and went back to Aziz. He huddled as if he was freezing. Then he talked about some men from Asia who had come to aid the Bosnians in their fight. They couldn't speak the language, but they were fierce fighters. Aziz said, 'Hell, it's like they want to die. Sometimes they bare their chests and hurl themselves out, and come back all bloody.'

'Really, who are they?'

'I don't know. Blokes told me they came to aid their fellow Muslims. These men, they frighten me. They look like Chetniks, behave just like those butchers. The other day they killed five Chetniks in one go and then cut off their heads. Then they took pictures of the heads under their boots.'

'Dear God. Why?' I rubbed Aziz's shaky chin with my nails a little until he calmed a little.

He pressed his eyes with his knuckles. 'My God, Fatima. I don't know. Our blokes are terrified of them more than the enemy. The worst thing is, we're getting used to it. At first I couldn't look them in the eyes and now we sit and eat together. I feel bad Fatima, I feel so bad. I wanted to kick them in the guts when they rolled those heads.'

I shuddered and stuttered, 'You have to ask for transfer.'

'Where? There's not much to choose. They put us where the Serbs attack, that's it. We're only trying to hold them back.' He fell on his pillow. I kissed him on the eyes. He pushed me off.

'What the hell, Aziz?' I yelled and hit him in the gut, but my fist bounced against his hard stomach. His face betrayed indifference. I hit him a couple of more times. He jumped up as if he'd woken from a bad dream and hugged me. Then he made it up for me for a couple of more lost nights.

Aziz's money dwindled rather quickly. We needed more cash. The army supplies were ridiculous. We took more from different charity organizations: Merhamet, Karitas, Red Moon, and Red Cross. I tried to find work, and asked around about possible ways out of our predicament. It didn't go well. People laughed at me and said, 'What can you do?' I said I could do anything and they guffawed or sneered or scowled at me and then simply turned away.

I went to Travnik twice a month to check the newcomers, and see if I could meet Aziz. I never did. Then, in early October, I got news about Mum and Father. Not televised or broadcast on some local station. A group of refugees from my town came to a gathering place in Travnik. I recognized a couple of shabby, hanging faces, but no eyes brightened when they saw me. They flinched a bit, as if instinctively wanting to tell me something, but they just passed on passed.

Then came a giant man sticking out of the stream like a rock. People glided and eddied around him. I thought I recognized the brittle chin and the squinted eyes. Father, I thought, and swam up to the little opening in front of him. I jumped up and coiled my arms around his neck. His voice was warm but distant, 'Glad to see you too.' I began to weep and he stood there, holding me with one arm. I wondered where Mum was, why she wasn't coming to embrace me, to scold me, but I didn't dare let go of him. I rubbed my chin against his stubble and kissed him on the eyes and brows.

I finally relaxed and he put me down. My throat froze and the only sound that came out was peeping. It wasn't Father. It wasn't Dad. It was just our neighbour, Selim. How could I see what wasn't there? He wasn't even as tall as Father. His lids opened and closed, slowly squeezing out tears. He looked straight at me. There was no way around telling me what I didn't ask in words. He whispered, 'I'm truly sorry.'

I twisted, shook my head and arms.

'The house was burnt down. They never came out.'

The words appeared in the air like rows of hanged criminals. I wished I could scream. I wished I could scream. I wished I could scream. I smacked my ears to take away the deafness, the silence. I clawed at my lips and my teeth and he seized my head with his huge hands. I flapped at his knuckles as fast as a hummingbird.

I fainted. When I woke up, I was lying in my cold bed. I had no memory of actually getting back to Zenica. Perhaps someone found Aziz, who then drove me back home. Perhaps I walked the entire way back, out of my mind. Perhaps an angel carried me on its back. I didn't have the faintest idea, and I didn't care. Selim was not there, nor was Aziz. I lay in my bed for hours before Aziz turned up with a bagful of food. I hurled it out the window. I threw him out too.

Was I infected with the survivor complex, as the women from Merhamet whispered behind my back when I tried to shove people from the line and get my food before anyone else? Was I cursing myself for those bad thoughts I harboured against my mum when she was ill and I left her? Goddamn sure I was. Not until I saw small dots, like a rash or some child's disease, crawling over my arms, legs, and breasts like red-ants, did I understand how much I missed them. I growled, 'Take this off me, take them off.' I rubbed my body with my palms, nails, brushes, forks, anything at hand. Aziz said, 'There's nothing there, Fatima. Nothing, you hear me!'

One morning I woke with my nails bitten to the quick and Aziz told me I'd been unconscious for two days. I was erratic for the next two. I spent Aziz's first long leave cursing him with words I didn't even know I knew. Nailless, I clawed at his face when images of burnt corpses flickered through my head. When two tarred faces lay in my brain like in an urn, I hurled accusations at Aziz. 'It's your fault. We left them left them. Damn you!' I cursed my lover for no reason except to release of my grief. I cursed and choked on my hoarse words until I collapsed again; then repeated the ceremony like a dogma. He never defended himself. He let me do to him whatever I wanted. Every time he opened his mouth to say something, to comfort me, to beg for my forgiveness, he gave up. In his own eyes, he was guilty and I let him take the blame that was equally mine.

I wasn't going mad. I was fading away. I knew it was time I did something. What brought me back a little was my piece of writing. It wasn't terribly journalistic, but it was a beginning. Indira, the woman who ran the camp, and who'd come by to inspect the conditions from time to time, told me the other tenants were complaining about my sudden outbursts, often in the middle of the night, then about my rudeness too. Indira said, 'The best thing is to talk about everything, over and over again, until every feeling is so watered down it isn't a problem any longer.'

'You mean with a head doctor.'

'Girl, there are no psychiatrists here. I mean a friend, a boyfriend. For all I care, you can tell it to a tree.'

'How about you? Will you listen?'

She didn't even answer that. Nobody listened to anybody those days. I had to tell myself how they died. Put everything down, if only to cremate the story. The pen was shaking in my hand as I wrote on the tablecloth in the first morning sunlight:

A moment after we left, three pipes, each hanging freely from a shoulder enveloped in darkness and contoured by the moonlight, entered the backyard of my house as if there was no fence and no gate, just a Welcome sign at the threshold. Thousands of sparks flew up, cracking from a torch and sinking into the crevices of the air.

A bottle with a burning piece of cloth hanging from it flew through the uncovered glass of the front door. Father and Mum jumped up from their bed. 'Fatima,' they yelled out. Two more cocktails were served. Smoke billowed. They shrieked, 'Fatima, Fatima!' and ran about, ignoring the flames and smoke.

Mum's hair caught fire. Father coughed, still trying to cry my name at the top of his voice. Then he burst out vomiting. Mum plunged into another furnace, the living room. She hit the bookshelves and the books rained over her. Father ran after her, took a cloth from the sofa, shook it to remove the flames from its corners, threw it on Mum's head and patted it. She fainted.

'Fatima, Fatima!' he cried, and ran into the flames in my room. His large body smashed the hall door open. 'Fatima, Fatima!' Cool air rushed in. The fire flamed on with ardour. But he didn't see three metal rings, casually leaning against the fence, waiting on the other side. A cracking sound forced Mum's lids open. Father's head hit the threshold. Mum was in her favourite room, amidst her burning volumes. The flames were red and yellow over the coal-black background of her things.

In feverish, frantic love, fanatical like that of Father Adorno, Mum opened the window and threw out the books. Fire didn't bother her. 'Fatima, Fatima!' The burning bookfall littered the ground on the other side of the house. As one large, green book hit the ground, it splayed open to the blank pages at the end and the last burnt gaze from its owner touched its smooth surface.

That was how my mother died, always herself to the end. That was how my father fell, like a tree trunk, like a country; the world should have shaken when he hit the ground with his flushed face. When his body melted and merged with the soil, the fucking world should've turned rancid and impossible to live in. It ought to have split and taken all the shit into the damn burning pit.

Lots of shoulds and oughts. None working. A bunch of broken tools, if you ask me. The story of my parent's deaths wasn't a story with my parents as protagonists. It was a story of reality, of tangible death, of burning and guilt and horror. Somehow, in this piece of text, they became any two people on this earth, anyone's parents.

The pen snapped in two sharp pieces and cut my hand as I reread what'd jotted down.

*

My grief changed with laughter. Out of thin air, I began remembering silly things about them, like that time when Father forced Mum to learn how to ride a bicycle. Father wanted a big, black German bike. He bought one called Crescent. I didn't have the heart to tell him it was a Swedish bike. He looked like he was riding a bull.

I never figured out why he insisted on teaching Mum, when he couldn't ride well himself. She, on the other hand, never managed to achieve the ideal eight seconds ride on the black bull and pass the test, so Father bought her a bright French bike. It was called Astra. Mum sparkled, pedalling a perfect straight line for six seconds, and then was tossed from her seat like a hen into a row of bramble bushes. It was spring and when we un-entangled her, her wounds smelled of fresh blossom. Father sold her bicycle cheaply the same afternoon.

When my rage and bitterness waned with the old moon and Aziz could once again lie near me and hug me while I slept without fearing another assault, he received his share of news.

At first, his sister-in-law, Weasel's wife, arrived alone in Travnik, to her family. 'Weasel's still hanging around back home,' she said, as if she didn't trust her own words, as if she didn't know what she was saying and meaning. But nothing about Behara and Ibrahim. She looked at Aziz as if he was asking her to betray the country (whichever damn country it was), and told him she wouldn't speak to him anymore. Every time he persisted in calling on her, she threatened to let the dogs chase him away. The animals only licked Aziz's palms, but he would walk away because he couldn't bear her ridiculously angry face. Still, he returned as often as he could, like a mongrel by a trash bin looking for fleshless bones.

All kinds of news reached him. He heard his parents were on the street and that his brother was in some refugee camp in Croatia, waiting for a visa to the USA. Once he even heard they were in Scandinavia.

Not until Elvis came to Travnik did anyone offer the 'They're all dead' version. Damn fucking shit altogether; stereotypes of war. These never felt boring and dull in real life. Never failed to surprise. Aziz almost punched Elvis in the head. 'The news is never certain,' Aziz said to me, rubbing his lips and chin with a handful of sand. 'You know, Fatima, you know, you know that man Rifet. They said he was dead and buried, you know, then the next day the rumour was he was alive and they said he was the greatest freedom fighter this country ever saw.'

That was true. The versions of Rifet's life didn't stop with these two. People talked about the man's unflinching struggle. Supposedly, the mere uttering of the man's name scorched the enemy's eyes and echoed like church bells in their ears. But no rumour lasted more than a week. Next we heard was that the man was a war profiteer, the safest job to have in a war, trading with the Chetniks and making good money out of the misery of his own people.

Anyway, Aziz believed Elvis. He had to. Believing in death was the easiest way out. Better to bury the bodies, even if only in your mind, than hope beyond reason. Ask women from Srebrenica. They knew better than anyone.

Aziz went on speculating and overusing 'you know' for a couple of days and then became mute. I couldn't cope with what followed. I'd known him to be depressed and gloomy, or silent and sad over many things, but that coldness was too much. Yet I should have understood him. I had regular fits, but he wouldn't react to those, or my caresses. Nothing touched him. He never said a foul word to me, nor to anybody else. Little by little, his leave of absences grew shorter. Even though he wasn't much of a warrior type, he demanded that he stay on the front line of defence. I didn't say a word about that. I decided to keep my grief to myself, just as he wouldn't share his.

Career Building
(Winter 1993)

The rest of 1993 burnt fast as pinewood. Early one November morning, I woke with a piece of Aziz's shirt beneath me. A large slice, chewed off with our dull scissors, which I found splayed on the sink, under our broken mirror. I thought, Seven years of bad luck. Good thing I'm not superstitious. I'd put his shirt under me to make sure he didn't leave without a kiss, but he probably didn't want to pull it out and wake me. What other reason? More radical interpretations came to my mind:

Aziz loved me too much to disturb my sleep.

Aziz wanted to cut himself off from me.

Aziz could no longer look at me.

Aziz was reluctant to kiss me goodbye because I had notoriously bad breath in the mornings.

The worst thing was that these interpretations didn't seem to exclude each other but worked together, like in that surreal painting with giraffes and melting clocks existing together in a flat desert beneath a sky-high mountain.

That breakfastless morning, Alma brewed some oats, which we called coffee those days, and asked me to join her.

'Did you see Aziz walking out this morning?'

'No, I slept like a bear.' She rolled a cigarette of dried walnut leaves in a piece of newspaper. The smoke was thick and dark. 'It's because of the paper.'

'What is?'

'The indigo colour in the smoke.'

'Ah, all right. Makes sense.'

She surprised me by asking, 'Do you know French, Fatima?'

'Not really. I'm not a polyglot, you know.'

'Poligut? What's that?'

I laughed. 'Someone who knows a lot of languages.'

'Oh, I quit school after fourth grade. Do you know any?'

'Some German and English. I had German in school and took some lessons in English too. Why do you ask?'

'I have a customer from the UN, a French bloke. Damn handsome, tall, always fresh-shaven and smells of pine cologne. His voice sounds so sweetly, but I don't get a word of it. He keeps saying pute, or puta, or something like that, when we fuck.'

I laughed.

'What do you think it means?'

'Probably some affectionate name, like bonbon or hot girl.'

'Ha, I like that. Makes sense.' Then she said with warmth in her voice, 'He gave me this poem but I don't know what it means.'

'Let me see.' She showed me. It was all Greek to me. I asked her if I could borrow it and find someone to translate it. I knew a French woman at Merhamet, where they gave out food, clothes, and soap. I thought maybe I'd make contact and see if she could help us get to France. Alma didn't want to part with the poem, but she wanted to know what it meant badly enough to let me take it. The next day, I took the note to the French woman. Some old fart told me she'd gone to another place and would probably not return any time soon. Pity. Yet the poem intrigued me, so I went to a local high school to see if I could find someone to interpret it for me. I found a teacher of history and philosophy who knew some French from his studies in Zagreb, back in the eighties. He looked like a scarecrow, but was cheerful. He had a slightly peeping voice. He looked at the paper a long while, then at me, and then finally translated it. It was called Alma:

> You were sleeping. I scarcely shut my eyes.
> Watching you beautiful creature sleep, snoring,
> your head against my arm,
> my forefinger under your necklace.

> My night was one long intensive reverie –
> that was why I stayed.
> I thought of my nights in Paris brothels,
> a whole series of old memories came back,
> and I thought of you, your dance, your voice
> as you sang me songs that were for me
> without meaning,
> even without distinguishable words.

My God, was the Frenchman in love with Alma, so he wrote her a song? For a moment, I wished I were that girl, a loose woman saved by a distinguished man with no tighter morals. The same story as in *Pretty Woman*, the most charming and the most disgusting film I'd ever seen. In the end, beside the intimacy in the poem, the girl is nothing but an exotic toy to a French conqueror.

I was thirsty. My tongue was clammy and I felt the smell of my own breath. I had no money to waste on bottled beverages, and Zenica had no fountains or springs, or even a nice quick river. I went back to the camp and returned the poem to Alma with the meaning I'd learned. She seemed to have fallen in love with these words she fought to pronounce in her hard Bosnian accent, totally unsuitable for fine French. Her Frenchman came to our room, to her, twice more. Alma told him about me, but I didn't want to speak with him. There was the trace of a ring on his finger, and I turned my back to him and went on sipping my cold nettle tea.

He never came back after that day. Alma blamed me. She said, 'You chased him away. You used *sihr* to do it. You wanted him for yourself.'

She kept having customers at home and I'd go out on endless walks, or hide behind our curtain and roll a sweater around my head. Blind monkey, deaf monkey, mute monkey.

My roommate made a hundred Deutsch marks in less than fifteen minutes when yet another UN observer came, quickly conquered, and left. The booty was not worth keeping, yet, so much money for a quarter of an hour. Alma was good at finding those who were loaded.

It took two hours for the line in front of the Merhamet quarters to disperse and for me to conquer three cans of salty camel meat, sent by some benevolent sheikh, they said. How very exotic.

I opened a can of meat and gave half to Alma, to break the silence. She sat on her bed. I crumbled my portion and ate it morsel by morsel. Alma took her half and munched it in four bites. She licked her fingers and leaned on the wall. I stared at her, my mouth hanging.

She laughed and said, 'What is it?'

'You like this?'

'I've swallowed worse things.'

I gave her the rest of the meat.

I lay on the bed, peering at the ceiling, while she brushed her teeth with baking powder, which was supposed to be the best substitute for toothpaste. I thought, Mum, Father, I love you. I know no one around here and no one wants to know me. But what do you care? If you're dead and gone, you're singing with the childlike creatures with wings.

I said, 'Alma, do you believe in heaven?'

She gurgled and spat out water. 'Of course.'

'I'll probably be hurled into the fire pit.'

'You deserve it,' she said and guffawed.

'Screw you.'

Alma said, 'I hope I won't end up in the part of hell where all the Chetniks are. You know there's this joke about a bunch of Bosnians and Chetniks in Hell.'

'No, and I'm not interested.'

'It's so funny. They help each other climb the wall around the fire pit, trying to sneak into heaven. When a Bosnian makes it up the wall, another Bosnian grabs him by the ankle and drags him down, crying, 'And where the hell do you think you're going?"

'Oh shut up! That wasn't funny. That's miserable.'

She waved her hand and went out saying, 'Killjoy.'

In the evening, a handsome, uniformed foreigner came. Half an hour later, he lurched out. Alma slouched in her bed, kissing the rustling money. I jumped out from behind the thin curtain and darted after him. 'You call that service?' I didn't yell, but he heard me all right. He stopped. I had no idea what to do but I thought myself clever. I said, 'I can keep you going four times as long.'

He frantically turned around and galloped away to his Jeep. I understood. He needed to loosen up a bit, relieve the pressure for a moment. I went back inside. Alma was sour. Not until an hour later did it dawn on me I'd actually attempted prostitution. I went from freezing to hot to freezing, like my mother when she grew old. Was there something in my nature that made me do it? I was a smart girl. Was that the best thing I could do? Or was there some dark, familiar itch in me?

The next morning, I got three more cans and some damn bitter tea. Then there was no humanitarian aid for a week. I rationed everything, planning for months ahead. The camel meat was fatty, salty as hell, and lasted a long time. I compared all other meals to that. God bless the sheikh.

Two weeks after that, I stole a jacket and two tins. They read 'beef' on them in several languages, even Japanese or Chinese, but it could've been dog-meat for all I knew. It tasted like camel anyway.

After that I fucked a man as I would change socks. I earned a hundred Deutsch marks for half an hour with a Dutch reporter. My first wage. The trade was sneaking up on me. I was so numb. My brain was dull. I hardly remember it, my first day at work. I don't remember his face or the place we did it. Were we alone in some motel room, or behind some tent? Perhaps we did it in his car in the nearby woods. But one thing I knew, I earned that money. It wasn't stolen, and the following week, the customer returned. And the week after. Those two times I remember well. He was bulky and his teeth were like snow under dark lips. His mouth smelled of dry saliva and his chin of some heavy, unfamiliar aftershave. He had big eyes and a clean-shaven head. He was fast. They all turned out to be fast. Not Aziz though. He was never quick, either to come, or come back from the mountain.

Then one evening, he called and said he'd be home in three days. I ran to the city the same night. I waited outside a store until it opened in the morning. I was going to spoil us for two days. I bought a chicken, ten peppers, a bunch of onions, salt, red paprika, potatoes, a pile of sweets, and a bottle of wine. I wanted to taste wine. I had no idea what it was like and wanted just a gulp before someone kicked the chair from under me and left me dangling.

I put everything except the chicken on Aziz's side of our bed and didn't leave the room for the next three days. On the third evening, I set the table, because Aziz was coming home. I wondered if he had any trouble, if anyone had discovered his double-sex. I assumed he'd tell me. Alma walked about with a sour face while I played chef. I had a dull knife and dull nails, which I didn't hesitate to use. It was bizarre. Was I going to meet him with an ear-to-ear smile and tell him I finally got a job? I wanted to. I wondered if I should get pregnant. Maybe he would desert that damn mountain for the baby. Maybe he would talk to the baby, that silly baby talk, ghuu-guu-guu, la-la-la. Lullabies. Sure. Why not? I hadn't heard a nice word for so long and we hadn't made love for...I lost count again.

Alma didn't put up any competition that night. She went out, but I never had the chance to say, 'Surprise surprise surprise.' Aziz didn't turn up. I ate alone, sat at that round table built for one and a half people, slowly chewing the food, every bit, before the dawn. I emptied the bottle, inch by inch. Everything still tasted like camel anyway.

*

Five hundred Deutsch marks later I went to Travnik to meet Aziz. He was supposed to be on leave for a month. He promised. He said the Chetniks were calm and hadn't attacked for some time. They were expecting a ceasefire. I found him leaning against the grizzled minaret in the middle of the old Ottoman ruins above Travnik. It was an old, isolated spot we'd found during our time in the town, and which we both liked. I kissed him all over his face and whispered my love like a schoolgirl. He didn't flinch. He'd become like that place – nice to see but no longer for living people. He stood and gave me a half-hearted hug. The autumn sun was strong but the light was like a thin fog. I told him about the money. I told him about everything. I hugged him and kissed his throat but didn't ask for forgiveness. Was he expecting me to? Did Scherezade ask her king for forgiveness? Did the king beg her?

Aziz only said, 'Let's go home.' I stared at him, but I didn't dare push him to see what he thought about it all. We went down the slope. Farther down, we ran into his mountain comrade Ziki, a bald, bullnecked, and bearded man. It looked as if he was having an argument with the invisible man. 'Motherfucking country and the arsehole politicians and their motherfucking children abroad, bathing in money. Fuck the warmongers and war vultures who make money while we're lying in those fucking holes like fucking maggots.'

We stood beside him for a while. Aziz asked, 'What's wrong?'

'What's fucking wrong? I'll tell you what's fucking wrong. We're fucking going back up there.' Ziki spattered Aziz's face with spittle.

Aziz didn't wipe it off. 'But I got off duty this morning.'

Ziki hollered, 'Who the fuck cares? I paid a whore up front, if you'll excuse the language.' He turned to me. 'They're making us get back before I've fucking fucked her. Fucking Chetniks.' He waved his hand at Vlasic, where they were stationed. 'They fucking decided to shoot now and for the whole past fucking week, they were playing us music.'

Aziz's lips closed on each other like the fast-healing opening of a wound. The upper whiskers merged with his lower beard like a closed zipper. Then he said, 'Fuck it,' and attempted to go down the street. I could hardly move, after hearing him curse.

Ziki took him by the collar and pulled him back like a dog. 'What the fuck do you think you're doing?'

Aziz pushed him back. 'I'm fucking going home, you piece of shit.'

Ziki's invective was more like an exhibition. It didn't mean much. But Aziz's words stabbed me between the shoulders. For a while, Aziz stood next to me in silence; then Ziki approached him slowly and menacingly, eyebrows raised and breathing fiercely through his nose. He grabbed Aziz by the collar. 'I know you feel fucked-over too, but just don't fucking treat me like the fucking enemy, capiche?' He let go of Aziz and walked away, saying, 'I can't fucking believe this bloke.'

Then Aziz called, 'Ziki! I'm coming. Sorry for that.'

'It's all right, mate; you're not yourself today,' Ziki said as he sprawled his right arm around Aziz.

They went off without a word. Aziz left me without so much as turning around and wincing, waving, or whispering. I went home like a zombie. I didn't care if I bumped into people, or if cars nearly ran me over, nothing. Aziz was stolen from me. When I wasn't well, he was here, but when he broke down, he wouldn't let me be with him. He just became empty. He was stolen from me.

Back in the camp, the tips of my fingers rubbed the slightly frayed edges of our passports. I wondered what use these were at all. We had never even reached a border. Passports went with borders. I said, 'You're just fancy little notebooks,' and put them in a small drawer between our narrow bed and the long, thin curtain that divided the room. I thought about the camp and how perfect it was. I had to believe it. It was no longer first aid. We had running water and a bed and a sheet and a blanket and a pillow and a tobacco-ochre ceiling at which you could stare yourself blind and walls with ears, but better than being on the street again, or in that wretched gymnasium in Travnik with hundreds of stinking feet and screeching children.

I went out and turned towards the peak I could see from the camp. I knew it was not Vlasic, where Aziz was stationed, but it was all the same. I didn't care about the logistics of warfare. I yelled at the mountain like Ziki, 'You whore!' My voice weakened immediately. I was screeching at the top of it, but could hardly hear myself. I tried again, 'You insatiable cunt! He mounts you day and night. You took my man and turned him green like you are. Simple green and black under the nails. You don't even feed us. You take and take, and you devour like an animal, like an old bitch with hanging teats, growing fat yourself. Where's our food? I'm hungry too. For bread and for someone to snuggle up to, for someone to talk to. Hungry, you hear?'

My throat became dry and I couldn't open my sticky mouth. I thought, At least he isn't violent, like the lot around here. He's silent and I can lie on his knees and listen to him sleeping. Maybe he's just too damn tired to care, because you won't let him sleep, ceasefire or not. You keep him awake, sun up or down, rain or snow. But he no longer talks to you: what it's like, how many he kills. It's hard to think of him that way but he's on the front line of defence. He can practically smell the enemy's feet, if they take their boots off up there.

I mustered some strength and cried feebly, 'Do they? Do they take off their boots when they mount you, bitch, or do you let them keep the leather and rubber on, for an extra thrill? Do they rape you, or do you rape them? Do they kiss you first? He doesn't kiss me, anyway.'

Sick to death with muttering, I went down to the city market and felt stupid because I'd forgotten it wasn't open on Fridays. I roved the neighbourhood. Not much to see on a drizzly day, but loonies who liked to waddle in mud for the sheer fun of it. But I wasn't out there for nothing; I just didn't know what it was, where to look or how to look. Chatter drew my attention. I spied for its source. A bevy of youngsters was looking up at the sky, laughing. One said, 'Nice rainbow, man.' I looked up and muttered, 'Not another damn rainbow.' Still, I loped in the direction they said the rainbow was. I knew there never was any point in it, just as poor Nisveta hadn't believed in it either. There was nothing else left to try, so I ran.

When I stopped to catch my breath, I was standing next to a bus stop, still a woman. I wondered, what if I just stepped onto the first bus, what would happen? I had no money with me, as my money was under a loose slab in the floor. I could stow away. At least I'd be on my way to somewhere. I laughed at myself, but the laughter expired. I wasn't in a stinking romance, with all the well-worm tricks and turns. Only, why not? I thought. Maybe the bus driver was a slave trader and would take me to a sheikh's palace. That was okay. There was a lot of camel meat there.

How about a white knight? Oh no, no more warriors out on missions to save the world and shit. First they saved a woman, fitted her up with a bed in a room with shutters on the windows, and then they pulled out to save another maiden in damn distress. I liked ordinary serendipities: a regular man with a job, working nine to five, home at nights, smooth hands. Civilian, of course. Smile like Aziz's, big and shining, homely.

Imagination doesn't count. I once learned about this Greek fellow who believed the world existed only in his head and walked around as if nothing was there unless he believed in it: no holes in the ground, or thieves with knives at his throat. Talk about loose screws and stuff.

Brakes shrieked. A big, black tire splashed through the water at my feet. I stood on the little piece of asphalt that did for a bus stop, my clothes soaked with the thick liquid that had splashed across me and now ran freely from the top of my head, and down onto my breasts. I hissed, 'How fucking typical.'

Someone hit me on the shoulder. 'What the hell are you doing, girl? Move!' It was a female voice, raspy. I pulled a wry face at the clammy perfume and then retched as a waft of cigarette smoke clouded my head. Then a big fist took hold of my right arm and pulled me aside. I couldn't see his face well. I wriggled from his grip. 'Hey! Stop that!'

He let go of me, but produced a tissue and wiped my face clean, moving upwards, nudging my nose and ruffling my hair. I looked up. 'You!'

'Ha, you,' he said.

I pushed him. 'Don't do that again.'

'You remember me?'

'No.'

'I know you. Fatima, right? And you just recognized me.'

'I didn't.' Of course I did. The handsome blond was Damir, Aziz's old army chum from our first trip to Banja Luka. 'Well, I know you, too. You're the kind who pushes girls around at bus stops.'

'Sure, only not all girls.' He appraised me. 'Incredible. You haven't changed a bit. Just as pretty as ever.'

'Bullshit.'

'That was a nice touch.'

A man wiggling a reeking cigarette butt with his thin lips and black whiskers pushed me back and made his way through, calling out, 'Hey, lovebirds move it!'

I said, 'We're not lovebirds, you old fool.'

I turned to Damir. 'I have to go.'

'Please don't. I'm just surprised to see a familiar face. It's been a while since I stumbled into you, but damn it girl, this war hasn't bitten on you.'

I hesitated and pressed my lips together tightly, as if not to reveal the thumping in my breasts. I felt like vomiting. Was it phoney serendipity, or some honey-bunny sweet shit? Can't men ever say anything of consequence? Something real? Something that would last? I pressed at the hole under my large T-shirt, where a normal stomach used to be. I wasn't having another false-appendicitis attack, but it felt like one. The old churning. I said, 'Who the hell do you think you are? Got to go; my husband's waiting for me.'

'Husband? You're married. Foolish me, of course you are. Old fellow Aziz, right?'

I nodded.

He sighed nervously. 'Let me tell you something, girl, you're all soaked and muddy, but you're still sexy. That's a good quality, especially in business. You'll have no future with Aziz.'

I said, 'I don't buy that cheap talk.'

'Okay. I'll tell you what, there's a cafeteria near here. Let's get a cup of coffee and some cake, for starters, of course.'

I sneered, waved my right hand in front of his face, fingered the air, then turned around and walked away from him.

He called after me, 'I don't buy that, girl. Your hand hasn't seen a rumour of a ring.'

I stopped and gawked at my palm, turned my hand and stroked along the ring finger, pressed hard with my fingertips, tried to find the treasure, or at least a slight mark. I couldn't wrest a single memory of taking vows, receiving a proper ring, wearing it, chatting about it with girls, not even having to sell it cheaply for food, nothing. He knew my hesitation and pounced on it.

'Come, please. I know you're tough but you don't need to lie. Let's get you dry and eat some.'

A big-breasted blonde with a skirt that hardly covered her missing knickers slithered up. 'Damir,' she purred. 'You're here. Fantastic, honey.'

I lifted my worries from my unwedded hand, made it strong again. 'Fuck off,' I said, but remained nailed to the ground. He pulled a piece of paper out of his pocket, came to me, put it in my hand, folded my fingers over it, and went over to the woman. She tried to kiss him, but he pushed her off.

The note had an address in Germany on it. What the hell's this? I thought. Does he think I can just take a bus and come round for coffee? Bullshit. I put the paper inside my bra. The area around me was full of houses, people walking by, and children playing. A moment ago, there was nothing there but the bus and the travellers. It was teeming with unfamiliar faces, and boisterous sounds. I breezed back home, thinking, To hell with love.

When I got back home, surprise surprise surprise: there was soldier Aziz, smiling back at me, his fellow soldier Ziki at his side, holding him by the right arm; a piece of chopped branch under his other arm; a bandage on his left thigh and a patch of blood on the dirty gauze; the leg slightly bent so as to not touch the ground; a movement, two short jumps on the good leg. I looked more closely at the wound; the trousers were torn but it was okay. Aziz gazed at me, waiting for me to come and take over from Ziki. I squinted. I stood still, but then rushed to support his weak side, helped him inside the room while ignoring Alma's sneers. I closed the door.

December 1993. Same country. Same war. Same camp. Same room. Same roommate. Same tension in the stiff air. It was freezing outside and not much better inside, either. Aziz snored and his bad breath competed with the icy suffocating smell of a man and a girl making too much noise for me to sleep. I whispered to Aziz, 'How much longer will he go on? That's not my experience of men. What's wrong with this old pervert?' There was an expensive camera on our kitchen table.

I'd had only two customers that month, both of them at the same time. As a beginner, I didn't know blokes wanted to do it together, like some half-gay stunt. They didn't pay much, but introduced me to two other blokes who could take me out of the country and fix false papers to the States. I told them Germany would be just fine, because I knew someone over there. I told them his name. They looked at each other and laughed.

Aziz knew about everything and said not a word. Madness! I'd rather he beat me to my senses, or ridiculed me, anything but behave as if all was hunky dory. He stashed all the money I earned in a hollow brick just behind our bed. We seemed to be scrimping and saving, but we spoiled ourselves with no more than one good meal a day. I grew more doubtful of Aziz. It was as if he were a half-pimp to me. He didn't mind, so didn't that earn him some such name? Everything was too damn weird. And he spoke of having kids. What the hell was going on behind those thick eyebrows? He had uncanny, and yet harmless and bland looks. His hair was still black as ever and shiny in the sun but his white eyebrows swallowed light. He didn't look much like a hero-soldier, but then those people considered to be real heroes don't look particularly strong.

Alma had two heroes. 'Not such sturdy performers,' she said. 'Nor payers.' Nobody got rich in the hero trade.

The man was still panting. A light beam coming from an uncovered corner of the window shone above my head, straight from the moon. It looked flaky in the soft darkness of the room. I whispered to my lover, 'He's getting there.' All of a sudden, life no longer felt so bad. At least Aziz was at home and he was mine to take care of. I was finally used to the washing and changing and comforting and working and making tastier nail soups; I was used to all the fornicators paying visits to our too-damn-cheerful roommate, and me. To all the perverts who came over to buy a piece of me like they'd buy a hot dog, never bothering to take off their rings or wash their hands and mouths afterwards. I never turned tricks at home: I did it in cars, alleys, once in some ruins.

I studied Aziz, wishing he was as when we first met, sweet and strong, always landing on his feet, removing the dust from his trousers and coming to me. The way a girl's first love ought to be.

A furious cry rent the soft darkness and cut short my night reverie. 'Enough! Fucking enough!' It filled the room and the light went on as the screen between us fell down. A sweaty, hairy mouth spat and cursed relentlessly. 'I say it's fucking enough, you cunt. I'm fed up with you and that fucking snoring shit-hole.'

I bolted back and thrashed against the bed frame. Wedged to the wall behind me, I glanced at Aziz, who mumbled, 'What in the world was that?' It felt good to hear him speak spontaneously, until the man jumped onto our bed and hitched Aziz up like a piece of trash, yelling at him. Alma joined the fight in a jiffy, as fervent as ever, her voice hitting me in shrill and sticky gusts. I could do nothing but stare and bite my tongue. Alma flailed with her thin arms, burying her nails in my tousled hair. I covered my face but the blows were too swift and erratic, like a hen with a fox at its tail. She took me by the head, and hauled me outside into drizzling rain. I lifted my face out of the mud and then Aziz's limp body fell over my legs. My head sank beyond the bottom of the puddle. The girl and the man bawled and shrieked, until their tongues were too tangled, their throats too dry, and they coughed and spat like smokers on early mornings.

A crowd of sleepy, pissed-off men and women closed in on us. Words of assault, colder than the winter rain, hit all the right nerves. There was a profound shortage of mercy in those days. The shallow mud opened deeper and deeper, swallowing us, along with all the discontent and frustration of all the world's refugees.

I woke up in a shed, curled beside Aziz, water dripping on my head. Aziz was asleep. I couldn't find paper to jot my message. Instead, I took a nail and carved it in the wooden wall beside his head: 'I love you but I have to go.'

I left him without a kiss.

Welcome to Germany
(Winter 1994 – Spring 1998)

Some free sex and a couple of bribed gays brought me to Germany. The air was still rife with the remains of the New-Year celebration. In 1994, Germans were not the problem; blossoming as the war was until the mid-nineties, Germany took care of the bulk of the people from the Balkans, several hundred thousand, especially from Bosnia. To get to Germany or any other country, that was hard. For that, I'd spent a night in a luggage-size slot under a pile of liquor and cigarette boxes.

Once in Germany, I stayed more than a year in a refugee facility, not terribly unlike the one in Zenica. It was so bizarre to hear people only ever talking about returning. They couldn't shut up about Bosnia: its fragrant soil, the exquisite food they were missing, the people full of soul and genuine goodness (what we called *merhamet*). Then, when rumours circulated that the Germans would be sending us all back when the war was officially over, suddenly they panicked, 'What'll we do? Where will we go? My house was burnt down. Mine's occupied.' Things like that. The old, settled *Gastarbeiters* just shrugged their shoulders and tried not to smile to our faces.

As refugees, we had no right to work. We received food parcels and some extra money for other necessities. Two men bought work permits, but had to hide it from the other refugees, who'd gladly terrorize them for that. The men became double outsiders. They couldn't go and live somewhere else outside the camp although they earned money.

I once went to one of those gas chambers up in Dachau. A camp manager, Armin, took ten of us to see his deluge of guilt over the dark national past. It was quite cold and I got one of my stomach aches and spent half the time in the museum toilet. When I came out, the rest of the excursion group had disappeared. I went into a chamber, cringed in a corner, leaned on the cold wall and stared at the wet concrete. I didn't spend the night in there though. A guard came, flashed me with his light, and kicked me out of there.

I left the shelter late in 1995 in search of the only man I knew, Damir. I thought, What the hell, let's start somewhere. He was easy to find, even though the address he'd given me wasn't up to date. Many men knew him, and they all leered at me when I asked about his whereabouts, leaving me without a clue. Finally, two thuggish men were most happy to provide me with the information while staring at my breasts.

When I entered a bright building with a cracked façade in Garching, at first I froze, while a nasty feeling crawled up my spine. I walked up three flights of smooth stairs, then around a broken cage-lift until I faced an open door. The walls were flaking. It was as if someone had spilled dread over me, dread as tangible as vomit. I wanted to turn back. Two girls sat at the threshold. They were twins, like two drops of water. I trembled. They examined me curiously from under their pencilled brows and fake lashes. The one to the right was beating the time slowly with a plastic wand. An hour later I'd find out her name was Kitty. She was a bony and pale creature dressed like a fairy. She had lace gloves rolled down to her wrists, looking like soft bracelets. The one to the left giggled when I tripped awkwardly. Her sister tapped her on the head with the wand, muttering, 'Give the bleeding whore a break.'

Inside, the air was nippy. A skinny little girl was perched on the edge of a table, peering at herself in the mirror above the mantelpiece. It was broken in a spider web pattern. There was a bowl of dumplings at her side and another smaller one with cream. She cried something in German, smacking a large dough ball.

Damir came in from the balcony, talking on a wireless phone the size of a brick. He smiled his big smile. My body turned as cold as hell. I felt I was sinking back into that mud as when Aziz and I were thrown out of the refugee camp. No matter what I did, I was following the same damn tracks. Was that a sign? Did it mean I should give up dreaming and resign to my fate?

In a bout of honesty, I told Damir about my times in Zenica. He thought it was natural that I'd go on working for him. So much for reunions. Damir was a *Gastarbeiter*, not a refugee. 'I'm not like the other poor bastards,' he once said to me, with a tear in his eyes as if out of some sentimentality and love of his people. He had documents and could stay for as long as he wished. He didn't have to turn his body and soul into productive work and save as much as possible for a new beginning in a war-torn homeland.

Damir had a partner, whom we never met. His cut was about the size of the regular German income tax. Only we didn't enjoy too many benefits. Lots of customers came through the other man. We pleasured some in a room in the Frankfurter Ring. The rest of the time we hooked in our cars.

In 1996, the papers said Bosnians would be *geduldet*, tolerated, throughout the summer. It's never easy to rid a country of some three hundred thousand refugees, especially when we weren't the only immigrants. That spring I felt like an illegitimate child left at somebody's doorstep. The whole of Germany was an orphanage.

Besides molesting the camp manager Armin, I was in trouble for pinching a couple of family jewels from a local German man, who had leather boots up to his knees, and clean-shaven head. I wasn't arrested at the time but there's a file somewhere with my picture stapled to it. I looked ugly in that picture as I do in my passport.

Two and a half years after finding Damir, on International Women's Day March 8th 1997, the news reported that another fifty Bosnians were expelled from the airport. There was a small riot by the Green party. The news anchor said, 'There are some twenty thousand more refugees from the Balkans to clean out before the end of the year.'

At lunchtime I got unexpected news about Aziz. Damir woke up rather late in the afternoon. His head was swaying like a stiff flag. He'd had quite a fight with a bottle of whiskey the previous night. He gathered all the weekly mail, whether it came from the landlord, the regular mail, or special couriers. He would always go through it on weekends. He made a bracer and sank into his special summer chair on the balcony of our new flat. We had to abandon the other flat because his partner had been arrested and Damir feared the man would rat on him. Outside, there was a small park with two tall juniper trees, a sandbox, three swings, and a large net for climbing in it. Six-storey-high buildings walled in the park like an oasis, as if they'd been built for the sake of the park and not the other way round. Not really a place you'd check for floozies. My colleagues, the twin princesses, were out shopping.

Damir threw envelopes on the floor, as he said, 'Bills, bills, bills.' Then he stopped for a moment twisting and turning a letter. 'I'll be damned.'

'Who is it from?'

'An old friend.' He read the letter, then after a minute said, 'Still nagging.'

'Can I see?'

He walked to the balcony fence and threw the letter. I stood fidgety for a moment, imagining the slow fall and the hit of the paper against the grass down there. I ran out to fetch it.

It was from Amila, Aziz's old friend. She'd once been in love with Damir, but he'd ditched her, as she had told me. Only years after that bizarre meeting with her, everything made sense. Back then, when she talked about Damir and his whores, I had no idea she was being literal, and not simply exaggerating her disappointment. Aziz's warning, which I had interpreted as jealousy, was the truth. Aziz had always cared for me, truly.

The letter was at least a year old, wrinkled and smudged, like an old piece of parchment. It must have been circling around until it miraculously found its way to Damir. It's possible to escape the police but not the post service or memories of old lovers. It was so uncanny to see it. Where had it been all the time? It was like that letter Father's sister had sent. There was no knowing how it arrived. Amila wrote:

Ciao
How does it feel to be on your own? Do you miss me? Just kidding. I don't care any more. I used to wake up at nights, shaking with desire for your kisses. I even dreamed of doing things with you that I said were disgusting, that I promised myself I'd never do. My parents and I are in Zenica and plan to move abroad, if we can get the papers from someone (I guess you wouldn't be kind enough). I hear Sweden is still taking refugees, and has decided to keep them there. Anyway, you know that girl Fatima who you said you'd seen a couple of times and that friend of mine Aziz, they eloped just before the Serbs killed her family, a nasty story. They ended up in Zenica, but then she left him, some say for Germany. You may even meet her there; it's a small world. Or she might be coming back soon. Aziz never left. I met him the other day. He's just as sweet as ever. I think I'll marry him. What the hell! I hope I won't be seeing you ever again.
Hundreds of kisses that you will never get.
Amila

As much as I was shivering because of the sudden cold wind, I felt warm around my ears thinking of Aziz's kisses and his big hands. Then the heat went straight down through my breasts and over my stomach and glided into my toes. I felt happier than I had been for years. It was one of the few generous moments in my life, I was happy for Aziz.

I was never attached to Damir and he knew it. He was handsome and cool for a while, at a distance, but the closer I came to him the nastier he became. I wasn't interested in love. I wanted an easy start. Boy, was I wrong. I tried to run away from him three times and every time I came back, penniless and tearful.

Since I'd decided to leave I needed money, more than the pocket change he used to give me. I stole from him a couple if times. At first, he said nothing. Later, he had me arrested to make sure I depended on his help to hide from the immigration police. That was the time I met Max.

I kept stealing. Finally, one night, Damir kicked me in the gut when I was walking up the stairs in our building. I rolled down the stairs and blacked out.

I came to in the bushes close to the zoo, Tierpark Hellabrunn near Flaucher Island in the south of the city. I heard monkeys laughing and strange birds singing.

I washed myself in the Isar: face, mouth, arms, neck and feet, the way I would prepare for a prayer, the way Aziz and I washed ourselves with the cold Lashva torrent back in Travnik. I thought of the time when I'd sat next to Nisveta in the mosque, trying to spot Aziz. I imagined stroking him between his legs, up and down, both his manhood and his girlish side, and he enjoyed it a lot and said he loved me, then said he loved me again, and said it once more when I fell asleep.

I looked at the clear sky and knew I was on my own. I tried to stay away from brothels: Westendstrasse, Leier Kasten just beyond the Frankfurter Ring, the 1001 Arabian Nights, only fifteen minutes from the central station. I wasn't welcome in any of these. There were few illegal immigrants in those houses.

I pulled some tourists into an alley and earned enough to stay alive for the first few weeks.

Ms. Kaytas took care of me. She was a little creature with short blonde hair and no make up at all. She gave the impression of a half-asleep fox from Russian stories, sly and ready to bite, even when she looked tame and kind. She used to run a place in Kreittmayerstrasse with a wall of fame, covered with pictures of all the girls she kept contact information about, which she would gladly share for a hundred Deutch mark, or some such symbolic price. The girls could charge at least ten times more. Munich wasn't a cheep place, but there were always immigrant girls that gave Christmas discounts all year round. Each and every one a good bargain. It was all a matter of how a girl sold herself.

Ms. Kaytas had all the best girls: models, actresses, and singers. I was lucky to be pinned up to that wall instead of a girl who had OD'ed. I was bruised between my legs and had huge blisters all over my back, boobs, and thighs. Damir had taken everything I owned: the clothes, the money I had stashed for a year to bribe myself a permit to stay, the Beetle I'd driven for three years; everything.

Ms. Kaytas said to me, 'I wouldn't feed you to the dogs.'

I said, 'I'll do men and dogs at the same time.' I didn't know if I could do that, even if I was forced, but I said what I needed to say.

She took my chin into her small hand and guffawed. 'You have something a little exotic about you, under all this.' With her hand, she drew a circle in the air around my face. 'But the 1001 Nacht brothel won't touch you with a bargepole.'

I hired a cheap cellar room in Swabing, and waited another week before my face was nice and clean, good enough to be eternalized on Ms. Kaytas' wall. Not a year later I asked my new Mum to let my light shine somewhere at the bottom of her drawer. I moved on again.

Epilogue

Strands of grass stand upright like soldiers in the setting sun. The night falls unaccompanied by police sirens, hollering men, and barking dogs. I amble out thinking sure I'm worth feeding to nice German shepherds, but none have come to sniff at my neck. I walk all the way down to the river Isar. It's a long way to go so I finally spot the strong stream early in the morning. I imagine the grass on the bank is soft Bosnian snow and I move my limbs up and down making new angels. I dive in with my clothes on. Washing before the final prayer.

Adnan Mahmutović was born in 1974 in Banja Luka, northern Bosnia and moved to Sweden as a refugee in 1993. He lives in Stockholm, where he is finishing a PhD in English literature. Adnan worked as a personal aid to a man in a wheelchair for 11 years. After his friend died, he took the position of a manager for a group of 10 people who take care of a teenager with special needs. He describes himself as "a Bosnian exile in beautiful and calm Sweden, the land whose naked north glistens with green Northern Lights".